EDITION 69

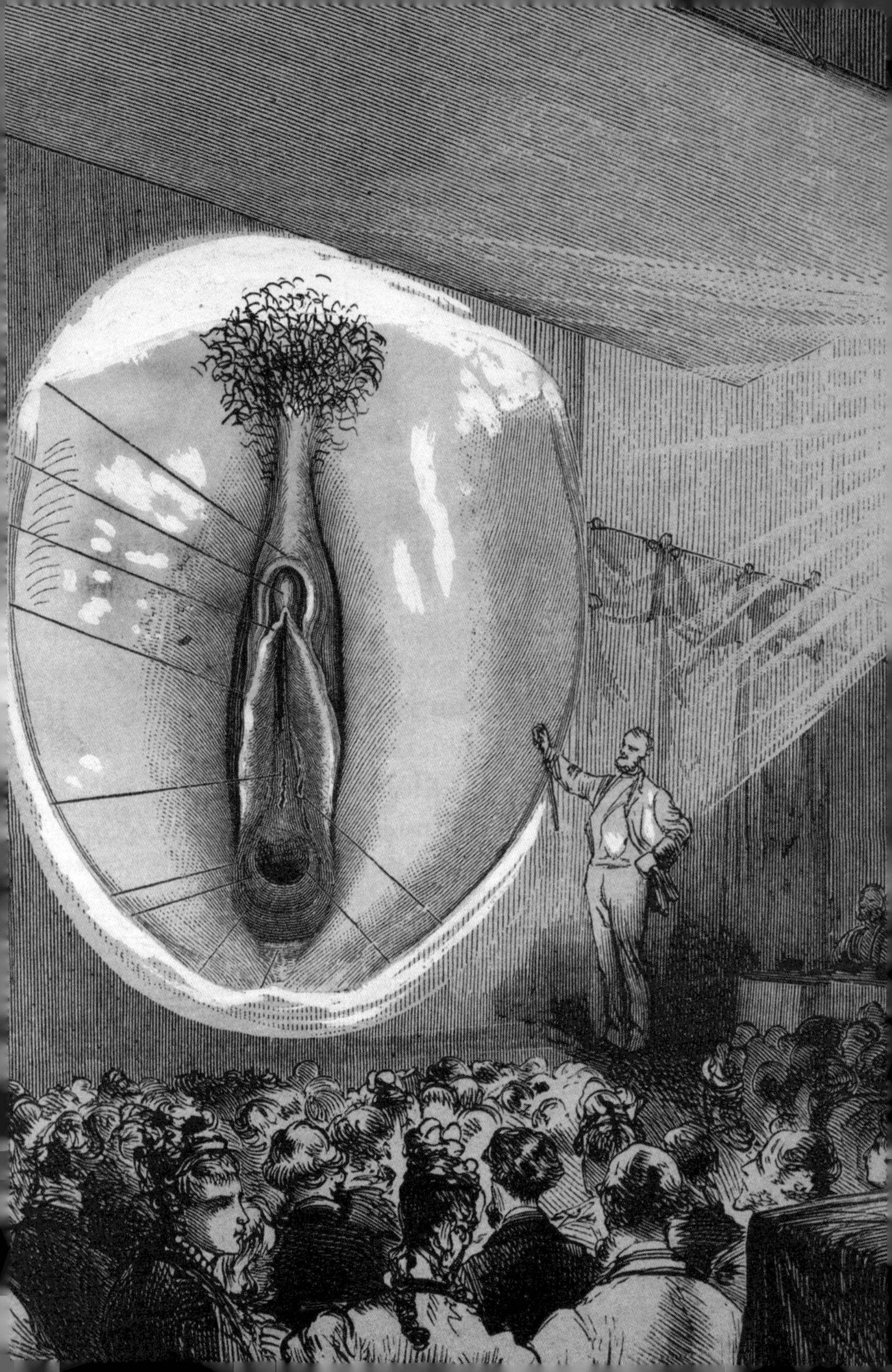

EDITION 69

FRANTIŠEK HALAS
VÍTĚZSLAV NEZVAL
JINDŘICH ŠTYRSKÝ

Artwork by Jindřich Štyrský

Translated from the Czech by Jed Slast

TWISTED SPOON PRESS
PRAGUE
2020

ISBN 978-80-86264-11-0

CONTENTS

Those who adore the poet Vítězslav Nezval will be captivated and thrilled by this unforgettable dream whose erotic terror transforms a child into both a lover and a poet. Sexual Nocturne *is an incarnation of the pervasive erotic and melancholic aura enveloping those sensitive souls who seek out moments of the Absolute. The ambiance of this novella — remarkable for its romantic and integrated unfolding of an inner life — is centered on a man who is experiencing through astonishing polyrhythms various stages of his life simultaneously. The central setting is the evening promenade of a small town and a brothel, which is also a bar under different circumstances and in a different time. Taking place as much in reality as it does in the author's imagination,* Sexual Nocturne *is a mosaic of images where ennui is condensed through the archaism of desolate street lamps, lunatic nights under a full moon, and floodlit bodies — the archaism of fetishism, garters, divans, makeup, alcohol, and the deep despondency of an insatiable sensibility.*

from the promotional flier for *Sexual Nocturne*

Vítězslav Nezval

SEXUAL NOCTURNE

a tale of illusion unmasked

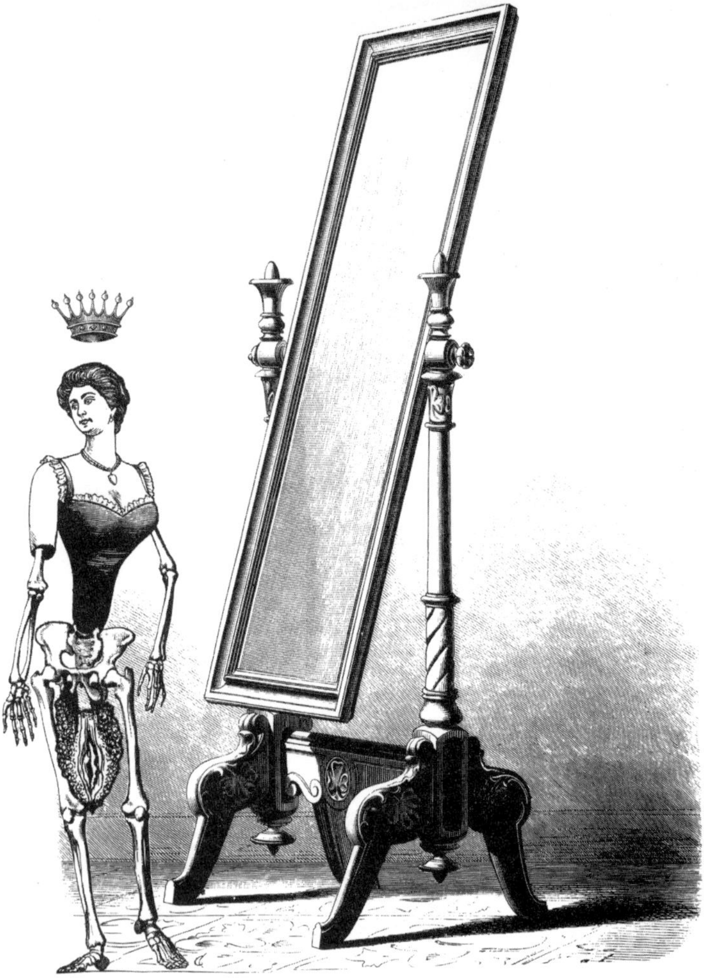

Nearly every year I take a trip to T. I should place the emphasis on "nearly" as *every year* is not meant to imply *stereotypically,* or *unavoidably,* or even *usually*. When I do go, it is almost always *unplanned,* not knowing if T. is my destination or if I will just be passing through. I was a student in T. from the ages of eleven to nineteen, and naturally I feel somewhat uneasy there — uneasy and marvelous.

T. is my Pompei, my legend.

If I take the bus, the countryside around T. is tinged with autumn. I see only wickerwork on the hillcrests.

Right below the station is a bakery where we used to hold spiritist séances. During the Great War, a dressmaker lived across from my room on the first floor. After he enlisted, magnificently outfitted Austrian officers would visit his lovely missus. Usually there would be two or three at a time, and they didn't bother to draw the curtains. The lady of the house would speedily get drunk and run naked around the room. She had long legs; I have loved long legs ever since.

I was fifteen years old, that is, at the age a woman's face is what a boy notices most. We want to be loved, and the eyes play the greatest role in this. Head after head insinuate themselves into our fantasies.

My fantasies already contained a fairly decent storehouse of heads. Encountering one on the evening promenade would set my heart pounding.

I trysted with heads, my emotions in turmoil. Before the town hall with its clock, in front of the bookstore, was a stack of cabbage heads nearly right under the arc light.

The square, shaped like a large U, was a parterre amid loges.

My heads moved back and forth only on the lower end. Their backdrop : HOTEL HABSBURG, a delicatessen, a watchmaker's, a clothing shop, The Three Stars Inn, a photographer's passageway, several dry-goods shops, a flour storage, a bank, and a toy store — the whole scene appeared cubist.

By the toy store a head was missing its amorous gaze. All at once it was January, or February, and the storefront was filled with sleighs and skis. Otherwise, if my heart just then hadn't been filled with such gloom, it was an autumn evening with rosy sunset and paper pinwheels.

It was pathetic to chase after these beloved heads. Standing in the photographer's passageway, staring in amazement at the promenade of women, I masturbated under my cloak. How miserable. I wasn't masturbating to bodies, but to heads, to eyes, and it dejected me.

Capturing the gazes of these disembodied women gave me a feeling of love.

How could I be anything but timid and desperate. I was so ashamed!

The clothing shop didn't exist, in a manner of speaking, and we shall see why at the end of this tale.

Then again, I never failed to stop by the watchmaker's where film posters hung on the wall. The ideal head was here.

There was also a peepshow. Once under the arc of a streetlight a little Jewish boy showed me pornographic pictures magnified by a watch crystal mounted onto a lighter. I was unable to untangle the Medusa of legs, arms, heads, cocks, and lips, and they would occupy my mind before falling asleep in my alcove.

I was apprehensive. The town-hall clock struck eleven, twelve, one. I crept into the kitchen and masturbated behind the maidservant's bed. It was awful. It was dark and quiet. This is how sexual murders get committed. Then the clock struck two. I fell asleep.

When I was twelve, I caused an enormous scandal. I was in love with an incredibly obnoxious, dolled-up girl from the town's public school. She always flirted with me when she came to my landlord's for singing lessons. I was fat, awkward, and acted like a clod, incapable of saying even one decent word to her. At the skating rink I fastened and unfastened her skates. Then I would skate a couple of

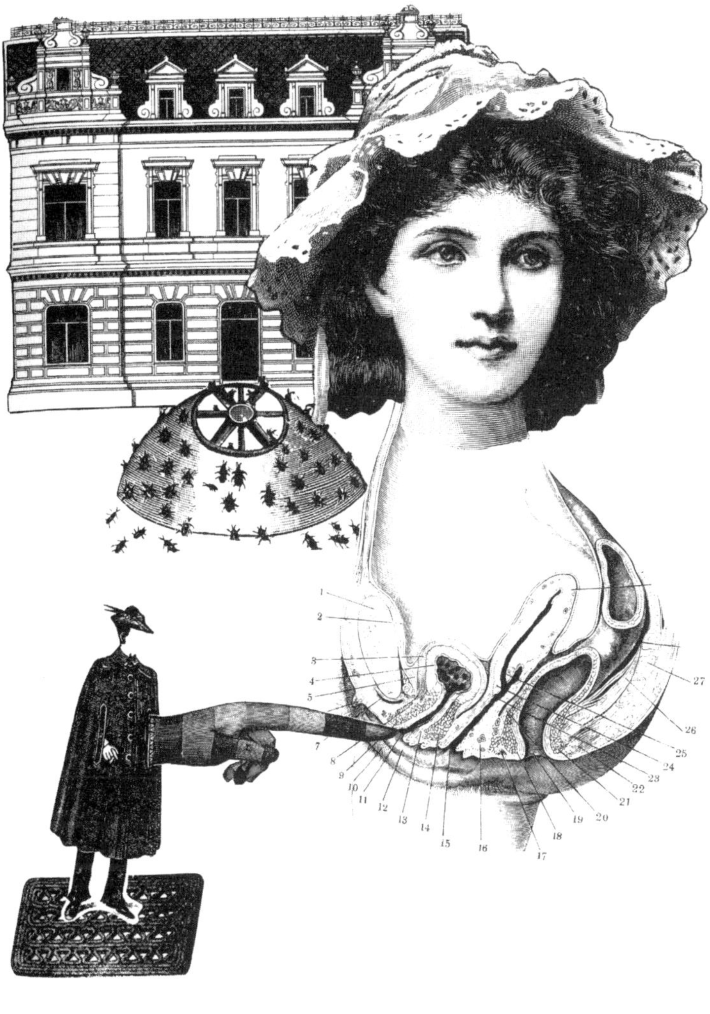
1
2
3
4
5
6
7
8
9
10
11
12
13
14
15
16
17
18
19
20
21
22
23
24
25
26
27

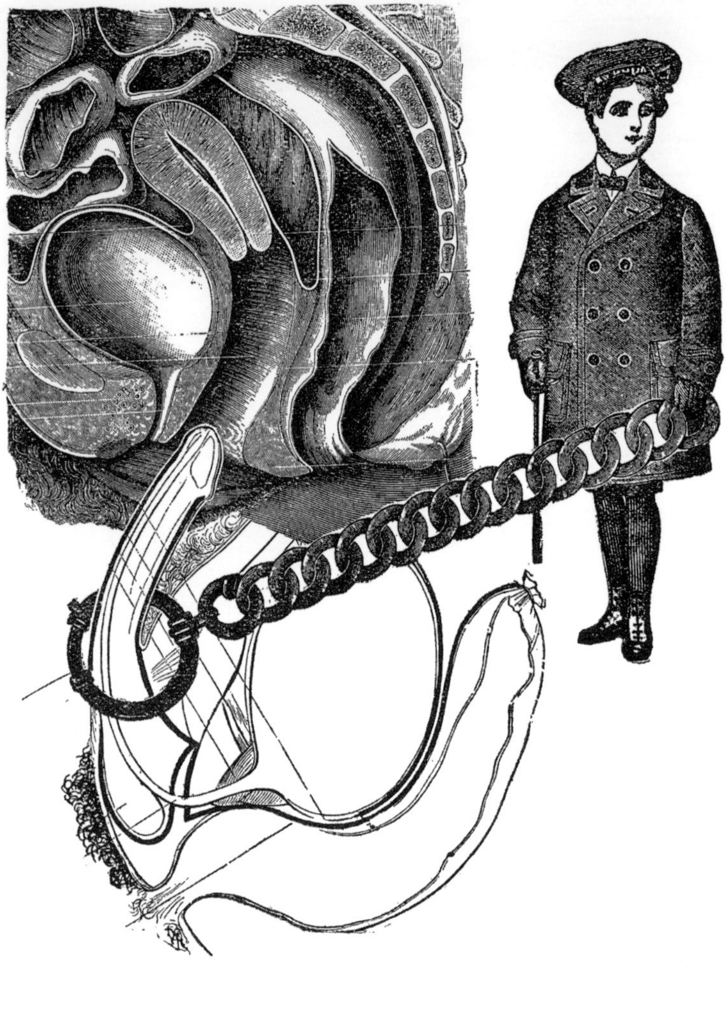

feet behind her while she shouted "dolt" at me. I had no idea what she wanted from me. She had about five or six girlfriends who were always with her. She would make delightful circles. During school vacation my grandfather came for a visit and gave me a one-crown piece. I used it at the stationer's to buy a porcelain doll with a rubber hat. It could be filled with water, and when the hat was pressed down it peed. I sent it to the object of my adoration. She replied with a note : "Do you understand these things?"

I sent word through her friends that I did.

In her second note she asked me how babies are made.

I wrote her back with genuine pleasure : "First you fuck and then after nine months a baby is born."

This is not a superfluous episode as it sheds some light on the relationship we have with words relating to the erotic.

The girls followed me from the skating rink to a secluded garden where they watched me take a piss. We agreed to go behind the cloister and I would show them how to fuck.

I was thrilled by the prospect. The girls walked behind me, but when we reached the square they ran off.

I wrote their princess a love letter in invisible ink. It was full of trite phrases. She didn't show up for our date.

Before even a week passed the catechist grabbed me before exordium and, shaking his finger, glumly ordered me to wait for him.

I didn't know why. Was it because I had pissed by the church? — Yes, one of the friars had seen me.

I was on the verge of crying. The catechist was fond of me; during religious instruction he pinched my cheeks and patted my behind. He was homosexual, but I didn't know what that meant.

After exordium he put his arms around my shoulders and asked what I had written to the girl from the town school. My knees went wobbly. I confessed to having written a love letter in chloride cobalt, of which I recalled only one stupid line.

The catechist was satisfied with this explanation. He stroked my head, my belly, my legs.

But the next day my landlord stopped me on the stairs and grounded me.

I waited for him until four o'clock.

He asked me about my little missive. When I said something about the chloride cobalt, he began to yell at me. He didn't care about the letter, but about what I wrote on that scrap of paper at the skating rink.

I'll try my best to reproduce his interrogation :

"Down on your knees!"

"Up!"

"Down!"

"Up!"

"Down!"

"Up!"

"Are you going to tell me the truth?"

"Please, sir, I was already questioned at school and the catechist has forgiven me."

"Quiet! Did she ask you anything?"

"It's not her fault, sir, I sent her an indecent doll."

"Describe it to me."

"It was made of porcelain, sir, and had a rubber hat."

"Describe it in detail or I'll give you a spanking!"

"Please spank me, sir. I bought it at the stationer's for a crown my grandfather gave me."

"Describe it in detail."

"This doll, sir . . ."

"Well?"

"It's indecent."

"What does it do?"

"Please, sir, it's indecent."

"Are you going to tell me or not?"

"Sir, it . . ."

"Well?"

"Urinates . . ."

"How do *you* say it?"

"Please don't make me say it, sir."

"Say it!"

"Pisses . . ."

"You pig!"

The landlord struck me and then shouted : "I won't

be the one to punish you, I'll leave that to your father."

Then he asked : "What did she write you?"

"She asked, sir, if I would tell her how a baby is born."

"No, you're lying!"

"How babies are made . . ."

I was mortified. There is a huge difference between "how is a baby born" and "how are babies made." "How are babies made" — the idiom "making a baby" is just a technical term whose brutality is revealed in deciphering its meaning.

"And what did you write back?"

"I won't say, sir."

"Say it!"

"I'm ashamed."

"I don't care. Tell me!"

After being questioned at length I gathered my courage and said :

"First of all, one must do shameful things, and then after nine months a baby is born."

My landlord burst into sardonic laughter and slapped my face, screaming:

"You liar. That's not what you wrote. I want to hear it from you verbatim."

I was about to faint. I couldn't imagine myself saying that word in front of a grownup.

My landlord insisted, and with such tenacity it seemed as if it were giving him pleasure.

I began to cry; I was sobbing and shaking. The landlord kept shouting at me :

"Say the word! Say the word!"

I closed my eyes, and in a daze I stammered out :

"First you fuck and then after nine months a baby is born."

The landlord gave me such a shove I staggered into the harmonium.

"Where did you learn that word?"

Several delicious scenes from childhood rose before my eyes.

I saw a primitive outhouse on a dungheap by the

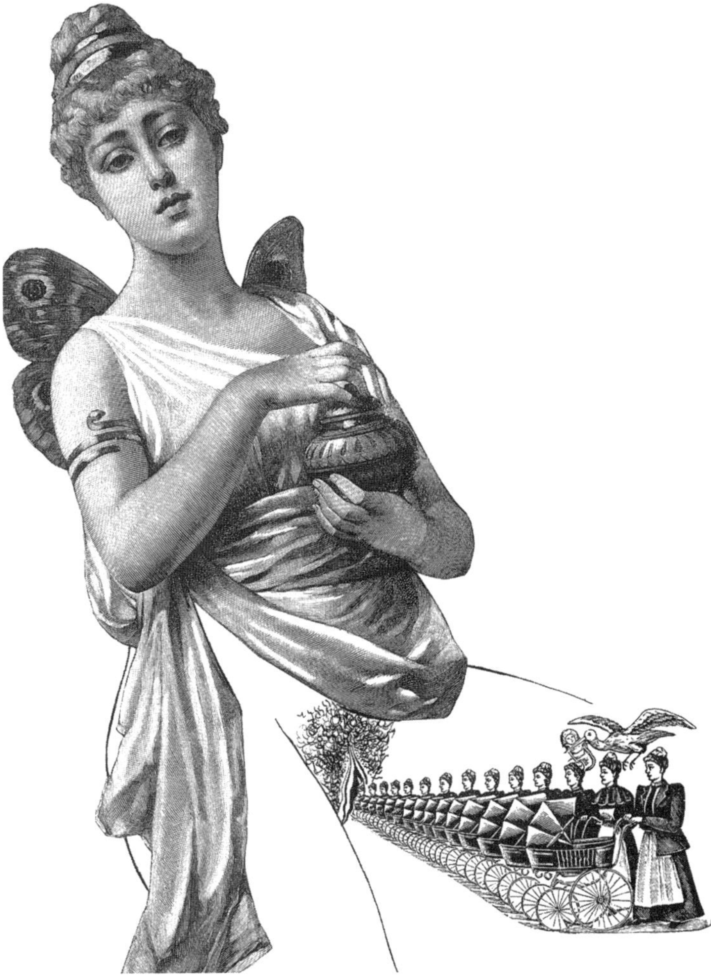

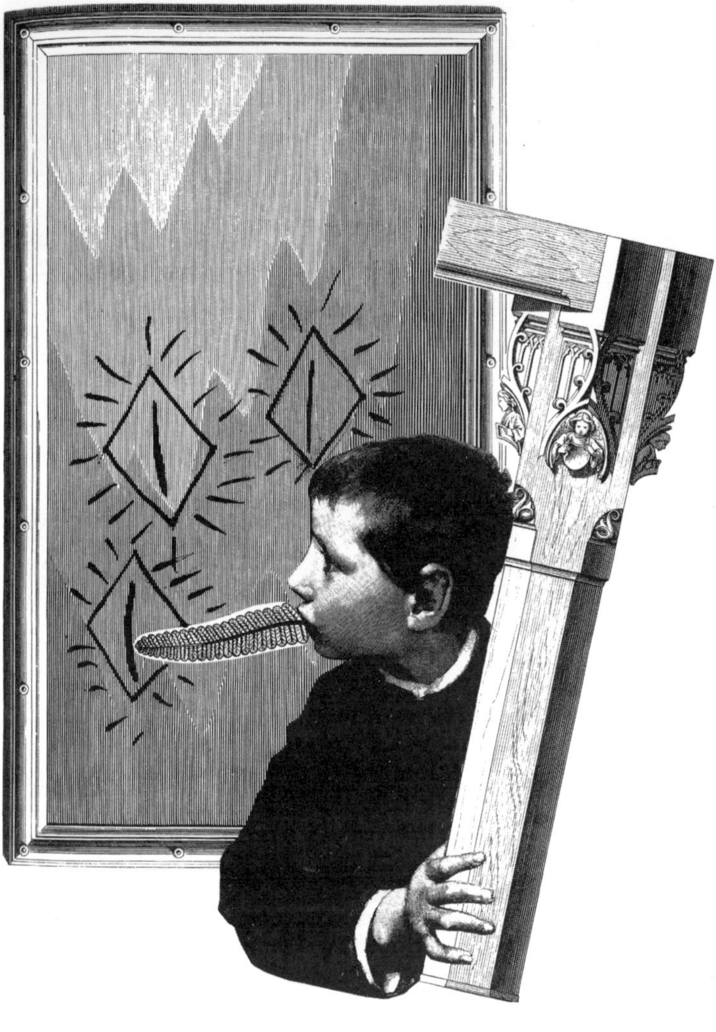

shoemaker's. When I was quite young I would regularly shut myself in this outhouse with older friends who were instructing me. Žanda was already able to come. He was sitting on the hole, squinting his eyes and jerking off. Then he squirted out a whitish snot. It was a wonder.

Then I saw myself behind the chapel among a group of boys. We were doing the same thing as Žanda. I was still too young and it didn't work for me. I was embarrassed.

At other times we did it in a tree amid the ripening cherries.

The landlord assailed me :

"Where did you learn that word, you degenerate?"

"From Žanda."

The landlord wrote my parents and immediately raised the rent of the lodgings. He wrote my father :

"For this act he used a word, the likes of which only the depraved would utter."

His views reflected those of society. How ridiculous. A writer is expected to make a fool of himself by employing periphrastic expressions while the word "fuck" is nonpareil for conveying sexual intercourse. Fortunately there are old dictionaries where this word has its monument. How I sought it out! When the kiss of lovers pronounces it during coitus it is infused with a sudden vertigo. I have little tolerance for its disgraceful and comic synonyms. They convey nothing, just mealy-mouthed puffballs that make me want to retch when I encounter them.

The word FUCK is diamond-hard, translucent, a classic. As if adopting the appearance of a gem from a noble Alexandrine, it has, since it is forbidden, a magical power. It is one of the Kabbalistic abbreviations for the erotic aura, and I love it.

I never utter this word in the presence of lewd women.

From the window over the bakery I watched the dressmaker's pretty wife fuck the Austrian officers. Her legs hovered gloriously directly opposite the window where, having switched off the light, I pressed my stiff cock against the pane. But these are just episodes to give the reader some idea of what an unforgettable atmosphere the town of T. held for me.

In T. there was a bordello. It had the archaic charm of a Max Ernst collage of etchings. One of my classmates was a frequent visitor. He was the café owner's son, and he wore patent-leather shoes and extra-wide pants. He stole things from home that he then sold at cut-rate prices.

Standing next to one another during gym class, we would talk incessantly about the bordello. I was unable to form a clear picture of what a pussy looked like. I just supposed it to be a very big hole, large enough to take the willy of a fifth former. My classmate laughed at me.

On the eve of May Day a witch burning was held in the park behind the cloister. The park filled with couples. The air sultry. I didn't have the gumption to hook up with any of the girls. In any event, I had yet to fuck one.

I watched the fire through the leaves during the interminable melodies sung by the choir of boys from the upper forms.

I said FUCK to myself over and over as I shambled along the footpaths with an unflagging erection. The whole of my desire fixated on two words : FUCK and

BORDELLO. Sensuality led me like a sleepwalker across the town square where two or three factory girls were hanging around.

I walked with my fly open, concealed by my cloak.

I went through the town gate toward the bordello.

Across from it stood the imposing house of the builder who constructed this quarter and gave it his name. The yard was strewn with several piles of planks and lumber.

Otherwise the entire street was unlit. A small lamp was on the bordello's façade.

My heart beat furiously as I debated whether or not to go in.

A few strokes of my hand and the urge would pass for the time being. But the thought of mounting a woman kept me from masturbating.

What if they throw me out? ran through my mind. But my friend from gym class always assured me that no one asked any questions here about your age.

I crossed the road. I buttoned up my pants and opened the door to the bordello.

I entered some sort of subterranean vault that reminded me of a butcher's icebox. The walls were perspiring in the same way. There were several doors; I didn't know which way to go.

A girl came out of the lavatory and asked me : "Do you want to go to the café or to a room?"

Terrified, I answered : "To a room."

If I hadn't met her in this vault and in virtual darkness I would have run off. She took my hand and, singing, led me up the stairs. All prostitutes sing. She sang an unintelligible operetta. I was walking past the café. Café. Café, mirror, off-limits to an eleven-year-old passerby intoxicated by the itinerant actresses. In those days they would sit from morning till evening behind the tilted windowpane. On account of these women, who from time to time would join the inane cicadas in sprawling by the window, I perpetrated a minor hoax.

I loved pharmacies, as if, surreptitiously through their fragrances, these women spoke and slept in them. Rumor had it that Miss Gerberová was syphilitic. I ran the stairs saying to myself : syphilitic, syphilitic. This meant : She sings too beautifully, she has knees, garters — she sings. After the performance she waits for her pay and has syphilis. Saying the word SYPHILIS made me delirious. It was a newly illuminated word : WOMAN. And what's more, I never stopped yearning to be allowed to ransack her box of costumes. Luckily she lived in an abandoned dump from where a few weeks earlier an eighty-year-old woman, who always frightened me on my way home from school, had been carted off to the cemetery. The crone was now in the grave and likely crawling with maggots and Miss Gerberová was living in her deserted flat where our ball would frequently land during soccer practice. I'll never forget that yellow mezzanine. For me it's the very same mezzanine where Raskolnikov murdered the moneylender.

The girl from the lavatory gaily sang her generic operetta ditty, and I had the feeling she was dragging me off to somewhere under that ruin. Budding potatoes sprouted along the walls. And like a flash of lightning I heard the flit of Grandfather's hatchet flaying livestock in the icebox.

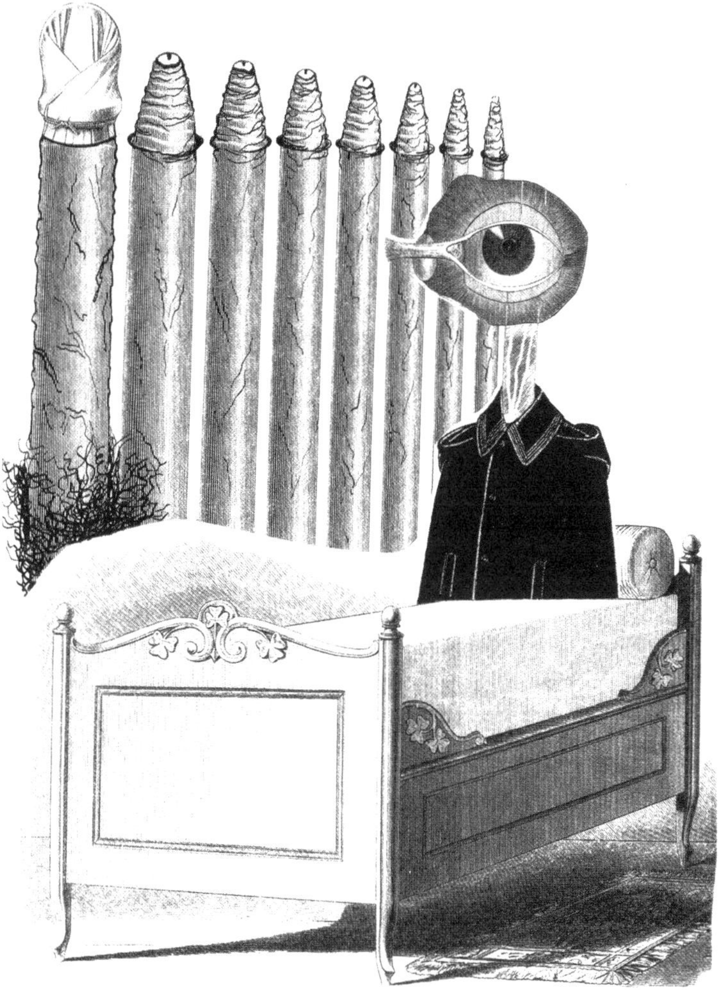

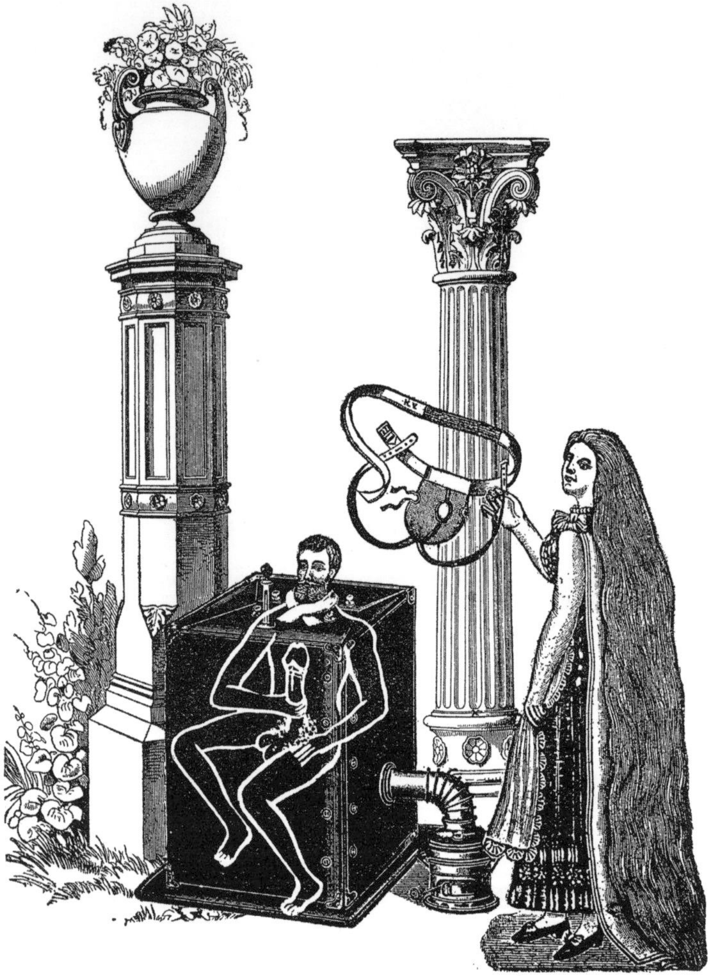

Around the sixth stair (I stumbled) there was light. The bordello's astonishing finesse filled me with dread. It reminded me of the time when I was no more than six years old and was looking at the illustrated pulp novel *The Prisoner of Angel Castle.* A dog seemed to come bursting out of the illumined alcove. But there was nothing. The place was exquisite. It was warm here, and suddenly I was no longer aware that it was from this window one could observe in daylight the stacks of lumber in the builder's yard.

Very few have been as keenly aware as E. A. Poe in "The Raven" of what an enclosed space signifies. This little den was completely isolated. The implication : the town's proportions had been altered. The room no longer abutted a cellar — it was completely isolated, like a small chamber whose precincts are only wind, a chamber overflowing with intense light, with a bust of Pallas Athena protruding from the wall, a demented bird swooping down on it. Yet this room had a mirror, which had ceased to be a mirror, a mirror-album, a mirror-novel. I don't know how I got myself across the threshold of this mysterious space, a description of which eludes me. I simply cannot describe it. A marvelous interior perhaps, the Dead-House from the most beautiful of Walt Whitman's poems. It had an inviting ambiance. An officious smoke hovered around the ceiling lamp. Something distinctly autumnal was present, a true autumn without nature, an autumn that is simply mist, seeking something more determinate than landscape. Apparently a lot of smoking had been done here. But this smoke, more likely exhaled from the photographs of the men than from actual cigarettes, made me certain that I was somewhere beyond that unreal world where fires burn and one is vaccinated for cholera. It was a very real room. The divan buoying my ass was so absolutely real and the absolutely real whore, now returning from the bathroom, threw off something like a chemise. She had on a type of dappled slip, and this roused me even though the raven had long been sitting on the imaginary bust of Pallas. I snapped out of it. The odor of theater wigs hung in the air. I said to myself : BORDELLO. Over and over I said it : BORDELLO, BORDELLO, BORDELLO, BORDELLO.

And in coming to my senses there also sounded way back on my tongue the word FUCK. Having just combed her hair, the whore poured a little water into the washbowl. Then she assailed my apathy. She sat down on the divan. I was once again overcome by an unreal nostalgia. I was at home in the attic flipping through a German edition of *Justine and Juliette*. The following titles appeared before me: *Rote Mühle, Zwanzig Marken Gage und eine Equipage*; Soulié's novel *Le Cadavre*. The girl resembled all the women from the xylographic illustrations in these penny dreadfuls. Once again I was impervious to the pullulating flesh of the whore beside me. The walls suddenly lost all ornamentation. The whore spoke. No sooner had her voice set the clock's pendulum in motion (now the room was just as inviting and comfortable as when I had entered) than I awoke from the cobwebs in the attic and my original intention returned to my squatting on the low wall above the builder's yard. My fly was undone to the last button. I felt shame. The girl nonchalantly settled herself on the divan, clearly in no hurry. I hadn't the courage to keep my body touching her hip. We were like two siblings sleeping in the same bed who create a space between themselves as they nod off. FUCK suddenly lost its meaning. My prick was pathetically shriveled. I desired nothing more than to be left there sitting amid the odor of theater wigs. Very few of the heads I had rendezvoused with on the square's lower end would have divested me of so many of my carnal thoughts as did this languid, absolutely somnolent head. Yet the girl wasn't exactly sure what was going on, and she made another attempt at singing something akin to an operetta. When I continued to cower, she evidently figured out what was wrong and said :

"You've never fucked before, have you?"

But now FUCK had the exact opposite effect than at any other time. It deadened all my carnality. All her uttering the word did was to make me aware of the speaking mouth, though giving this mouth a kiss was something I could scarcely imagine. The girl took my hand and said rather benevolently :

"Play with me, silly boy."

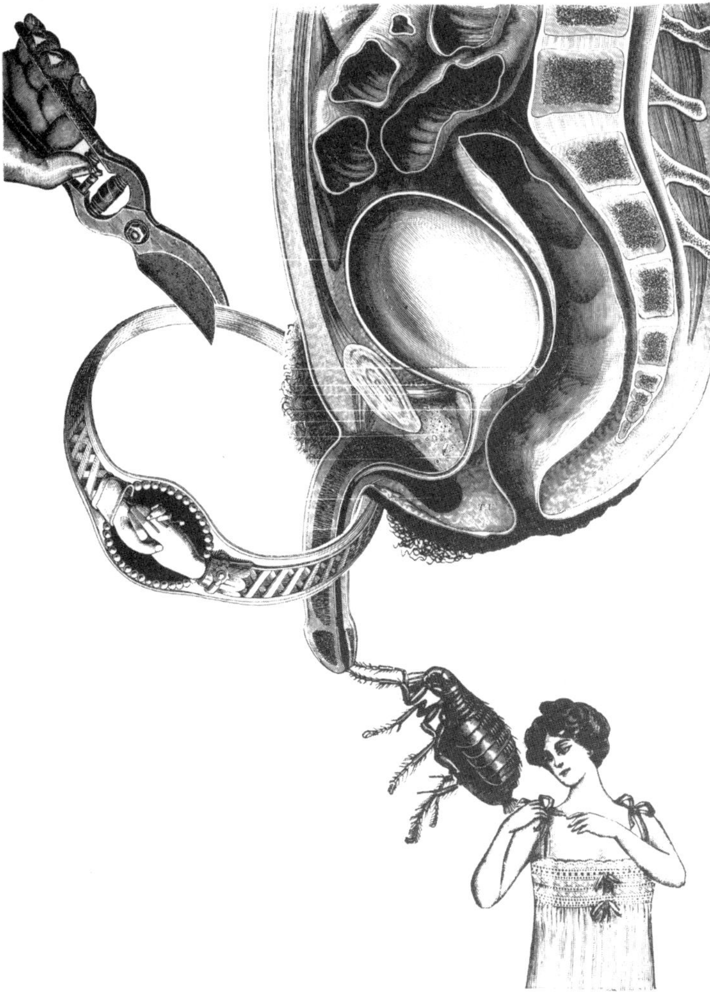

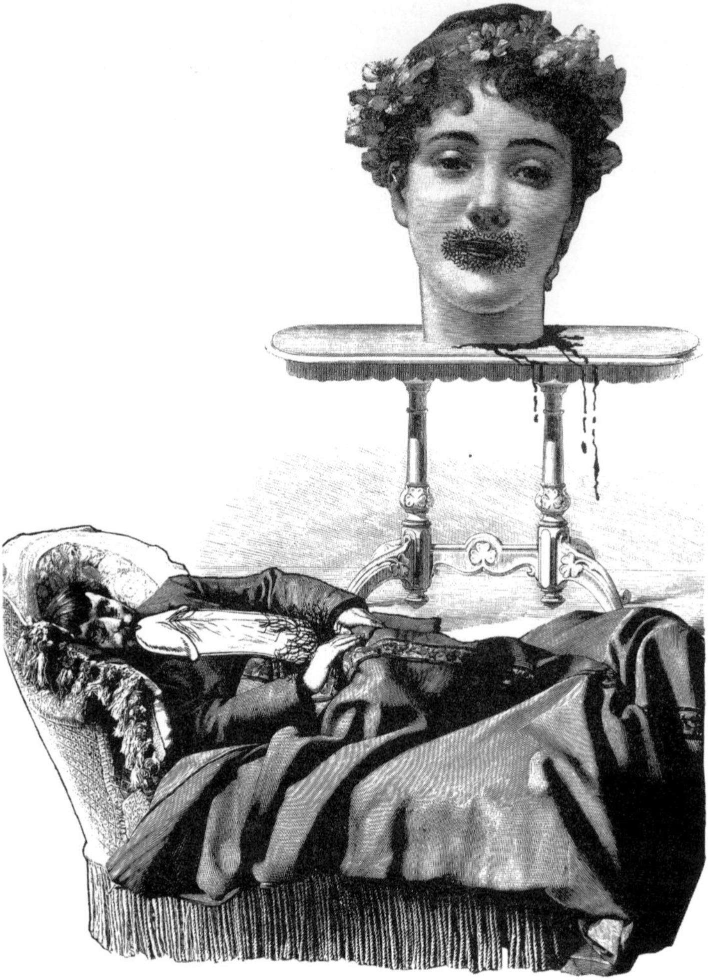

She removed her panties. This certainly roused me. Without any segue — and to many it would seem beyond all reason — I thrust my head into her pussy. I breathed in the same pungent smell with which the maid's dirty blouse had intoxicated me. Without segue, like a thunderbolt from a clear blue sky, my cock became erect. Everything at once changed. In that Poe chamber I threw myself onto the whore's body, my tongue falling between her perfumed teeth.

Her hand removed my pants. I plunged into her cunt, which was so unexpected and so singularly proportional. I dared not move. This was entirely different to the practiced hand under the cloak opposite the promenade. Her vagina engulfed me in a hot nonexistence. I was fucking. I was fucking and I spurted into her cunt, which itself was somehow moving like a slug.

I shouted out : FUCK, FUCK!

She said : "Hold on and stay a little longer."

I was ecstatic and would have gladly stayed like this forever.

If when I entered the room it had seemed cut off from the town where I lived and attended school, if it seemed to have emerged from the pages of an anonymous novel, appearing to me like an outmoded illustration, to such extent that the continuity of my intellectual life had been disrupted, its isolation now revealed its true essence. It became a room from a dream. I didn't know by what mechanism, through what trapdoor, it had emerged, imprisoned in the present and without future, in time without time.

I was the only male inhabitant with the only female inhabitant, serene, without any relation to past and future, exactly like someone climbing a rickety ladder in a dream, a ladder whose lengthier segments are simply replaced by a void. The clock's ticking, wandering in as if into the beyond, had the l'art pour l'art urgency of a prank, of a system gone haywire. And the delight I took in the naturalism of the wall paintings, photographs, wallpaper, and curtains returned me to the marvelous, to an atmosphere of surprise and materialization, to spheres of absolute sensation. I would have likely confronted the most heinous accusations with the insentience of a sleepwalker. In other words, I had a conversation without conversing, a conversation without its mirror, without its mark; I uttered words whose existence ceased the very moment they were delivered. And yet (after this total realization of dissociation) it was wonderful to sense behind those blinds, directly opposite them, the builder's jumbled yard. No longer its intrinsic self, the yard now served me, the same as anything else, solely as a means of contrast. And still, as if only the product of my memory, like one of a number of ephemeral details we latch onto in the morning after a deep unconscious sleep, the prostitute's face gave meaning to all this isolated chaos, which had stopped being chaos. What we talked about is not important. It was silly of course. But her worth, the worth of this room, so subjective, created one of those high moments that convinces us to put off suicide. Truth be told, I wasn't sure (not only after leaving, but even at that moment when I considered my being with her something as immutable as a crystal) if I would even recognize this woman if I were to run into her in town (I hadn't considered this), I wasn't even sure if she had a face, if she weren't just a generic abstraction. I saw no hope of ever working out the locus of this moment in the realm of my delirium. If I hadn't already been well aware that in life nothing changes, that is, no absolute changes, I would have considered my life to have indeed changed at that point. I saw things I had never seen before that day. The receptiveness of memory to dreams is no different. Of all the things I had encountered, I now recalled only those that meshed with the atmosphere of that Poe chamber. Now I enjoyed aimlessly standing around in the photographer's passageway. Through its murk, which I so liked to enter, I tried to make out the features of the photographs on display, feeling the need to transpose the known into the unknown. So on a Saturday I would stop in front of any pub that was emitting a clamor. On other evenings I would stroll under windows of no special importance with the certainty that behind them a one-of-a-kind performance was being enacted. I was fond of hanging around the stationer's shop on Sundays, and only on Sundays, when the shutters were down and all the absurd odds and ends behind the shop window were out of reach. I would clear a path for myself with a pocket light, and wherever I went, in my mind's eye I was forever and persistently entering the cellar that for me symbolized a higher unreality. In this way I learned to love the plumes of gendarmes, and coffins, the hours free of people, and clouds, which during the night demarcated *interiors* from *exteriors*. I nearly became a keyhole snoop. Walking with my eyes shut, I learned to distinguish the contours of reality by smell. I wallowed in the scent of the tailor's workrooms, and for no reason at all would seek out those parts of town that were least on my mind. If I wandered to some yellow corner, it was only because I had once seen it from high cliffs at a great distance. I ranged beyond the street lamp I had once seen from outside the hospital. And I always returned to the photographer's passageway, not having the patience to indulge myself in the pleasures of a twelve year old. One day I had my photograph taken. My portrait was not what interested me, what I really wanted was to capture my fixations. While being photographed I imagined my whore, though her visage had practically vanished from my memory and all that remained was just the idea of her. Yet no sooner had I relinquished the comb and the photographer's hand mirror (it was afternoon and a mule-drawn flourcart was driving down the passageway), as if a hallucination, I encountered the woman from the icebox on the square.

She looked beautiful and was beautifully dressed. Her gaze brooked no possibility of my making eye contact with her. She had metamorphosed into a head, into one of those inaccessible likenesses that filled the storeroom of my fantasies. Yet as she walked a swathe of her fragrance — which I caught hold of, which I caught as if a whiff of Corpus Christi — filled me with a deep despair. At the time, and perhaps for the only time in my life, in that extreme intensity, I could have seriously contemplated suicide.

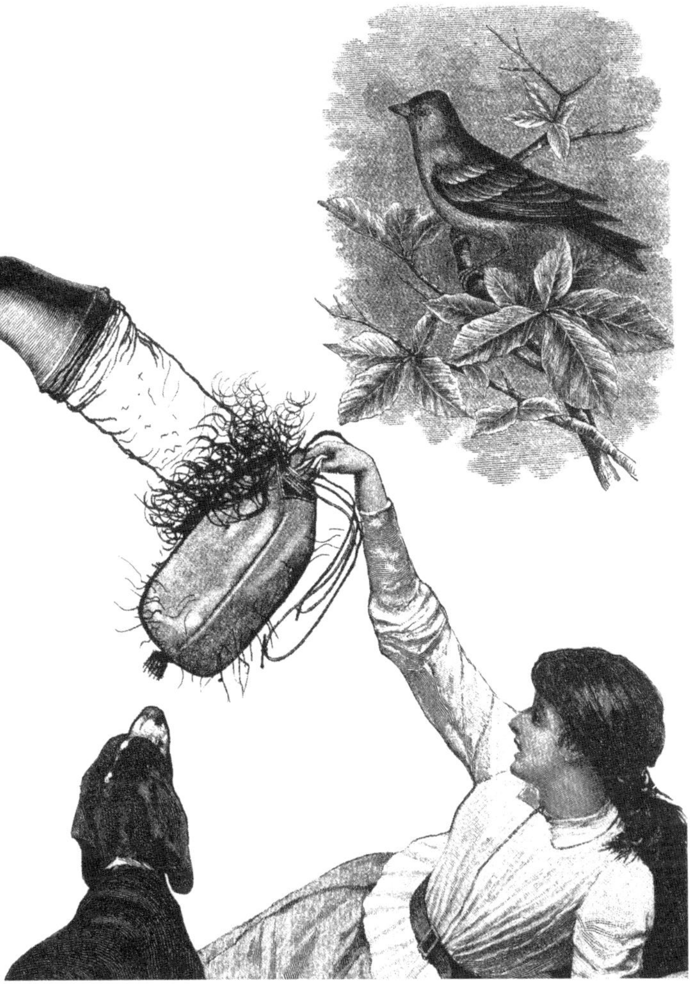

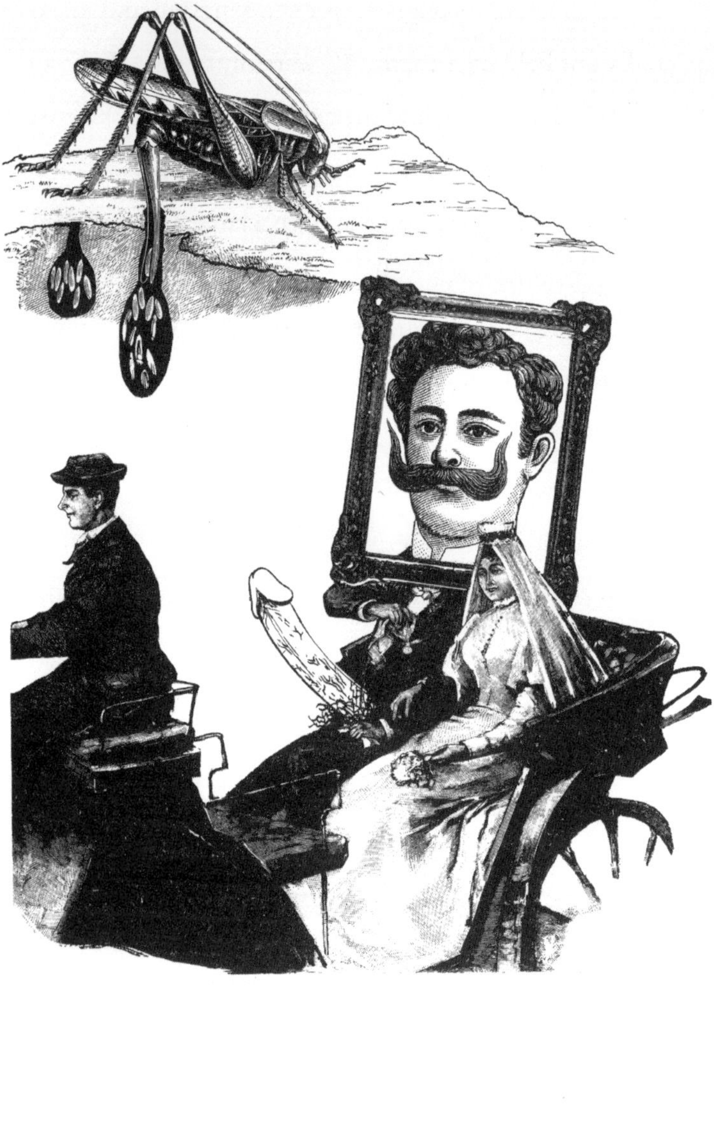

I was traveling through T. not too long ago and unexpectedly got held over there. We were in the café that had been off-limits to me while the town was still not yet part of my history. In the small hours we went to a bar. As soon as I walked in I forgot that I was with a large group of people. I don't know what pulled me in (a narrow rivulet, a black millrace, was flowing along the place) and I don't know why I took a seat at the bar, as this is something I usually hate doing. I was drunk. At a nearby table in the company of two older men who were just paying sat (like in a rowboat during a public celebration) a beautiful, hardy, thirty-five-year-old woman. She was the wife of the bar's proprietor, who had just graduated when I came to this town as a young student to take my entrance exams. Back then I sullenly sat with my grandfather in the traveler's inn. A tall house stood in front of the inn, crowded with large signs. One had the name of some wholesale merchant that ended with the letters USS. I looked at those giant letters like a moron.

The lady was the daughter of this USS merchant. As

soon as I laid eyes on her I fell madly in love. I sat down at her table. She said to me :

"I knew you when you were a child."

I didn't reply. I stared at her for an hour with the same lunatic gaze I had directed at those large letters. A band was playing *Auch du . . .*

A friend from our group joined us. He was related to the lady, who played the role of the establishment's prostitute. He said to me :

"Well, say something."

But she answered :

"No, don't say a word."

She looked at me, then said :

"Come again some time."

She rubbed her body against mine, and I said :

"I see your wedding."

In my mind's eye I was at the window overlooking the square, which was overflowing with a wedding. I saw a woman in a veil wearing a garland on her head.

I said everything to her in three words.

She gave me a gentle look and, crying, said :

"You won't come again, will you? Do come. Come after a few years maybe."

Again she brushed her body against me, and her tears dripped onto my face. Then she left and didn't return. I drank heavily. I lurched through the streets and broke a number of windows. I frightened a young girl on her way to work. My friend and I (miraculously) entered the traveler's inn, which had just opened. It was The Three Stars, and only a wall separated us from the clothing shop where my mother had bought me a cloak on the day she and my father brought me to this town, where I was to remain. I held my friend's hand. In my thoughts I was in the clothing shop. I have never freed myself from this sensation. I likely lost my mind there.

ORIGINAL COLOPHON

EDITION 69, VOL. I, VÍTĚZSLAV NEZVAL : SEXUÁLNÍ NOCTURNO. PŘÍBĚH DEMASKOVANÉ ILUSE

Designed and illustrated by Jindřich Štyrský. Published privately in autumn 1931 by Jindřich Štyrský, Křemencova 5, Prague II, for the publisher's friends and collectors in 138 numbered copies, of which nos. 1-69 are printed on Pannekoek Holland and nos. 70-138 on Simili Japan. Intended exclusively for subscribers and not for public sale, nor available for loan, neither in public libraries nor disseminated in any other way.

František Halas

THYRSOS

Not to be born is, beyond all estimation, best; but when a man has seen the light of day, this is next best by far, that with utmost speed he should go back from where he came.

SOPHOCLES

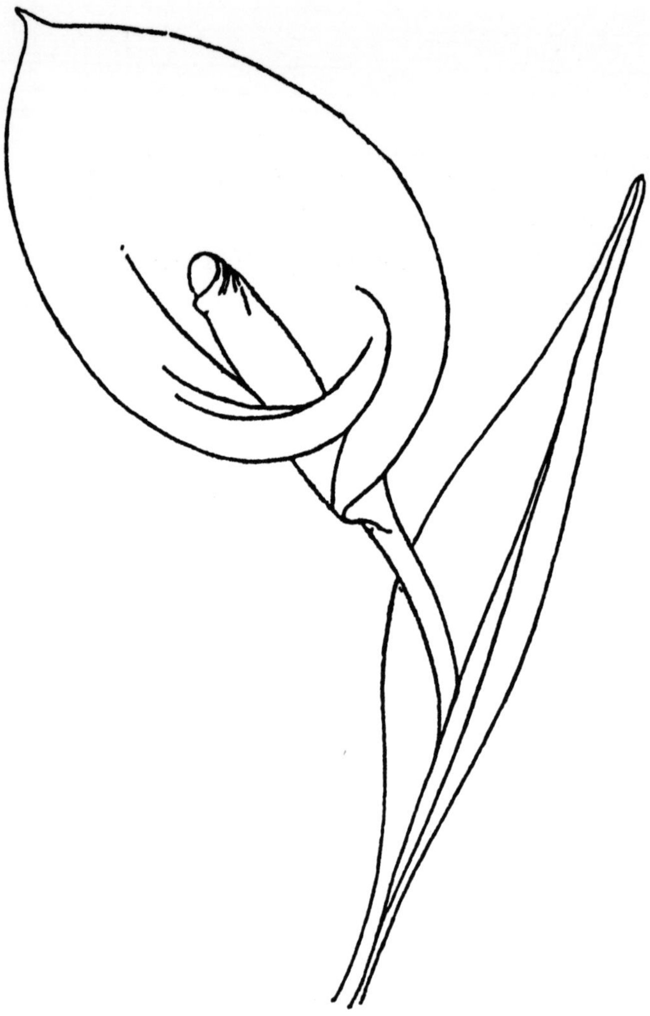

LEDA'S SORROW

O winsome swan my love's intense
yet forgive my desire to know
why your long neck is not below
a sign of your stiff concupiscence

THE TASTE OF LOVE

To have all vulvas spread open wide
and to kiss that warm alley they harbor
to taste a thousandfold yet never plunge inside
that familiar rose splayed to your ardor

Incomparable beauty of the mons
that ancient routine has you disdainfully vexed
it isn't love when on her breasts you lie prone
and grind her lovely flowering sex

The extended clit gently massage
take a long swig of that vaginal wine
drink until drunk on that rare vintage
more pungent in taste than any aged vine

We're gifted a tongue not only for speech
its key unlocks delight elsewise hidden
when lubricious spasms convulse a breach
adeptly slip your fingers all the way in

Pucker your lips in the shade of her pubis
let the mucous dew her petals of rose
the touch of your lips driving her delirious
until her rapturous skin blissfully glows

To have all vulvas spread open wide
then to stay there and sleep
to taste a thousandfold yet never plunge inside
only to suckle tenderly and deep

A SCENE FROM ANTIQUITY

Just the hairy hand is seen from the brush
the taut belly of a faun dreaming
gestures familiar and fingers twisting
a bacchante's hidden shade laughs in a hush

Oh his surprise as he feverishly shoves
through her lowered hair his little flute
that she deftly excites for his desire to shoot
and wet her prurient mouth with dewy love

Weary hooves sweetly batter her sides
and a curious hand roams her low and high
the naughty little urchin brazen and spry
inserts his horns where they should never reside

When her protestations has his tears welling
in mercy she again blows on his flute
naughty herself and acting resolute
she straddles the boy and savors his swelling

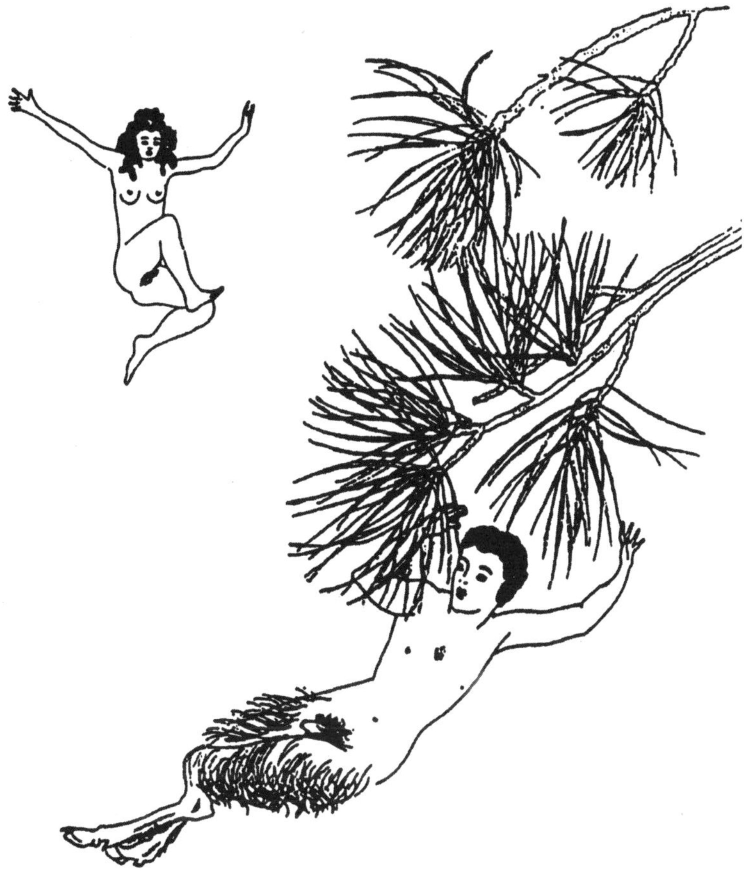

Night falls the flute's silent someone pants from afar
the weary faun's about to sleep soundly
she strokes it again and he shudders roundly
as she runs into darkness to an ardent centaur

Come morning and lo again plays the flute
he rises in tears and wanders the woodland
whispers and laughter from branched dryads offend
and livid he reams a tree hole to render one mute

ANCESTORS

Virtuous maidens in arcades softly giggle
at bulging sacs in elegant trim
fathers in maashauses undo flies with a jiggle
stallions' blood frothing viscid within

and the wives those able archers
with bowstrings in bed taut to limitation
spirited mares and wanton lovers
always in heat for a hot penetration

With the battle over soldiers cruelly violate
the bodies of women in villages seared
a slew of mongrels left behind to populate
sluts' cackling in the camps reaches the ear

Ancient ancestors hear our plaints
and of the lasses had and those now with us
all that throbbed for you for us is just faint
doing with a mouth what you did with a phallus

MAIDENS

All skin and bone and still flat
no shade under bellies to be seen
on their lips virginity stays redolent
numbed with fright at the monthly scenes

Repulsed by the boys who smirk
at their coupled hugging on a stroll
each one so ugly and a dense jerk
unable to fathom their love at all

Ensconced at home they playfully pet
bodies entwined with long caresses
drunk with pleasure from nubile pelts
and lusty kisses planted on their pale roses

Peaky eyes now closing as they lay
silently dreaming of who will be her first
their hair wipes the wet of limbs away
each smiling at her beauty in the glass

BROTHER AND SISTER

Dear sister sleeps as her breath lightly lifts
her tiny breasts with seductive charm
but sleep's not for him in a feverish fit
a jutting boner sheltered in his palm

Fearful he draws back the shirt from her belly
and bends over her in long hesitation
stealing glances she observes him well
afraid her dreams will have consummation

As if in sleep she deftly spreads her legs open
he puts his head between them down there
the tiny hairs his lusty teeth begin groping
overcome with delight and gasping for air

Tears of bliss and quick feigning of sleep
when spasms shoot all through his sister
he turns his back and she quietly weeps
that he's no longer kissing her little beaver

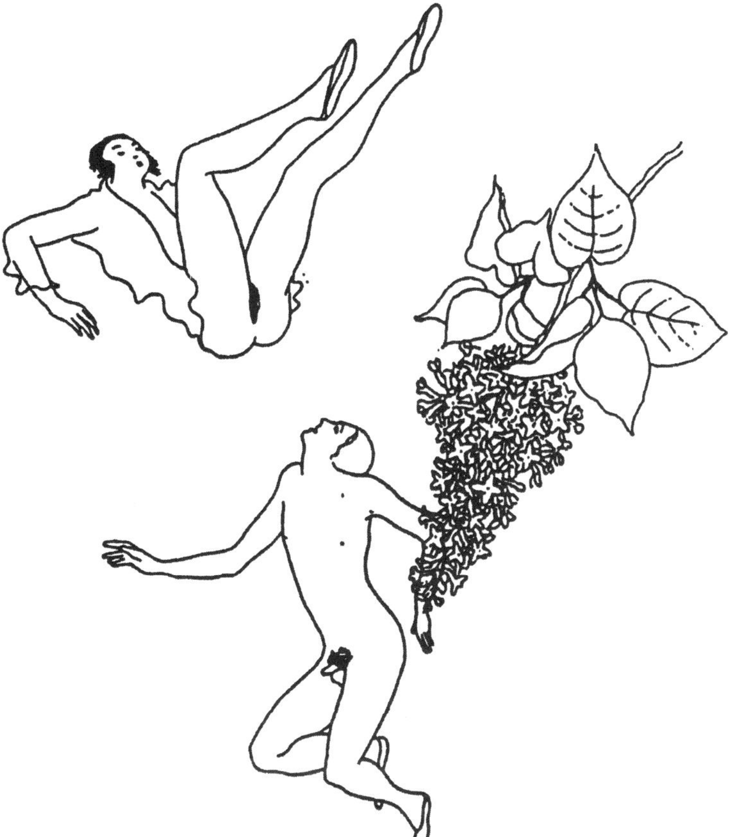

IN THE FIELD

There where rats hungrily squeak
and squelching mud the only strains
in battlefield trenches after the attack
where rack and ruin has its reign

where desire festers like open gashes
a heady smoke hovers over this lair
the soldier trembles and passionately thrashes
shaking arms embracing nothing but air

Then he unzips and jerks off like a demon
his cock nearly a forgotten appendage
he runs from the hole to death for no reason
women desired now phantoms of a mirage

and the whole trench behind him in delirious refrain
the living barbed wire at once an erect barrier
his sobs of passion fall silent in the prolific rain
only the grim rattle of dying comes from his cover

AN OLD MAN AND WHORES

From its nest the pecker has now departed
yet his rutting continues in rabid prurience
stalking the streets with a hellish appearance
startling a young girl peeing with legs apart

Grunting and jangling gold pieces he prowls
cathouses for plump whores to haul back to his den
to ride against their butts as he slides out and in
to the thicket where peckers are fowled

His fallen belly jiggles and shakes
as laughter peals over his flaccid state
if he randily faints their douche will resuscitate
and a towel of breasts wipe his drenched face

Red all over a stroke lays him low
they rob him blind and quickly escape
eyes rolled back and moaning mouth agape
for a round ass and a moist pussy to plow

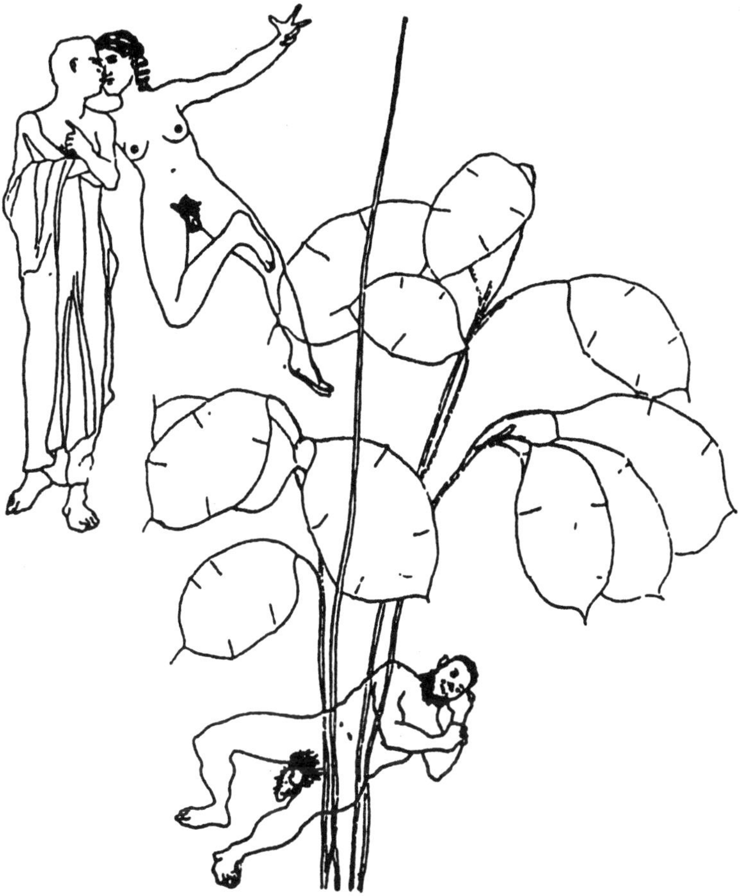

CHILDREN

On a trash heap in grass full of blight
children playing under a blazing sun grow weary
as murky shadows shower their clear sight

A child remembers a night of terror and dread
long awakened by cries and deep breathing
how he stared into the dark out of his head

Everyone now whispers together in a huddle
about what is disturbing their dreams at night
how their fathers and mothers so strangely cuddle

On her back one girl then lies down
and a boy tries to show in comical writhing
while the others aghast in a circle all frown

NAUGHTINESS

Enough of kisses enough of embraces
now for a new game that does not bore
be happy your prick is no longer bracing
as your other abilities can now come to the fore

Have her raise the heart of her behind
from your navel to your piehole
then slowly and gently realign
while still gripping your flagging pole

and in performing this deft equitation
suddenly press your lips to her clit
and whisper into her a silly recitation
until her entire viscera say I get the drift

SOUND ADVICE

In a pussy's sweet folds
be sure to keep in mind
next door is another hole
for your finger to find

Gently push it in good
lightly massage the breasts
and at once your waning wood
will become stiff as a mast

ORIGINAL COLOPHON

EDITION 69, VOL. III, FRANTIŠEK HALAS : THYRSOS
Designed and illustrated by Jindřich Štyrský. Published privately in autumn 1932 for the publisher's friends and collectors in 138 numbered copies, of which nos. 1-30 are printed on Pannekoek Holland and nos. 31-138 on Simili Japan.

An unwitting smile, a sense of the comic, a shudder of horror — these are the sisters of eroticism. The sisters of pornography, however, are always only shame and disgust. Some will look at these erotically-charged photomontages with a smile on their lips, others will be horrified. The author has complemented this series, whose essence is the moment of supreme pleasure, with a story that was once told him and has long haunted his dreams. His sole release from this perturbation was this attempt at iconoclasm — scissors are able to sever any form of inseparable double : male from female; sun from sky; death from the living; the dream from waking life.

from the promotional flier for
Emilie Comes to Me in a Dream

Jindřich Štyrský

EMILIE COMES TO ME IN A DREAM

Emilie quietly recedes from my days, evenings, and dreams. Even her white dress has dimmed in my memory. I no longer blush when thinking of the mysterious teeth marks I discovered one night on her groin. Those last pretenses impeding ready-made emotions have vanished. And lost forever is that entire chorus of girls with vague, nonchalant smiles when remembering their hearts burst open by passion and a humility semi-perfidious. I have finally rid myself of this face I had sculpted in the snow as a child — the face of a woman consumed by the compliance of her cunt.

I see Emilie cast in bronze. Those made of marble also are not harassed by fleas. The tiny heart of her upper lip recalls an old-world coronation, while the lower lip, accustomed to being licked, brings to mind the foliage of a brothel. I walked slowly beneath her, my head in the hem of her skirt. I saw up close the tiny hairs of her calves crumpled in irregular patterns under her fishnet stockings and wondered about the type of comb needed to straighten them out. I came to love the fragrance of her crotch : a mix of laundry room and mouse hole, a pincushion forgotten in a bed of lilies of the valley.

I was prone to seeing in dissolve : whenever I looked at Klára, I always saw Emilie's features, with her modest quiff. When Emilie was in the mood to sin her sex had the fragrance of a hayloft and spices. Klára's fragrance was that of a herbarium. My hand wanders under her skirt, touching the edge of her stockings, the snaps of her garters, stroking her inner thighs — hot, moist, delectable. Emilie brings me a cup of tea, wearing blue slippers. I will never again be completely happy. I am tormented by the sighs of women, by eyes contorted in convulsions of orgasm.

Emilie never tried to enter the world of my poetry. She viewed my garden from over the fence, so that such ordinary and natural fruit appeared to her as the terrible fruit of prehistoric paradises. Meanwhile I numbly shuffled up and down the footpaths like an idiot, like a wayward dog sniffing the grass for death and fleeing its destiny. I was madly seeking a recurrence of that moment when shadows settle on a particular town square somewhere in the south. Leaning on the fence, Emilie rushes through life. I see her clearly : each morning she rises with her hair disheveled, goes to the toilet to pee, sometimes to take a shit, then she washes with tar soap. With her perfumed pussy she hurries off to mix with the living to rid herself of feeling split.

Emilie's laugh was a marvel to behold! Her mouth seemed an arid hollow, but when your head was brought closer to that upper cavern of delight, you heard something inside her quiver, and when she parted her lips to meet yours, a piece of ruby-red flesh darted out from between her teeth. Old age likes to coddle time. Morality sleeps soundly only in pleasure's embrace. And her eyes, which never closed at the peaks of ecstasy, expressed an otherworldly rapture, seeming to be ashamed at the conduct of her lips.

In those places where I search for my youth I find curly golden hair meticulously preserved. Life is an incessant killing of time. Death daily gnaws away at what we call life, and life ceaselessly devours our desire for annihilation. The image of the kiss dies before the lips draw near, and each portrait fades before we even look at it. In the end even this woman's heart will have a worm crawling through it and laughing in its depths. Who then will be able to claim that you actually existed? I saw you in the company of a naked young girl, beautiful and breathtakingly white. The girl raised her hands to reveal palms black with soot. She imprinted one hand between your breasts while covering my eyes with the other in such a way that I saw you as if through torn lace. You were nude, shrouded only in an unbuttoned cloak, and at that second, I witnessed the whole of your life : you had the likeness of a swollen, rapidly germinating plant. Two stalks growing from the ground seamlessly merged at the very place you began to wilt and fade, but your body had already developed a navel, breasts, and head sprouting two lovely pink buds. Yet at this moment the lower part of your body shriveled and collapsed. And I, writhing in front of you, fingering the hem of your cloak, grunted with a love I had never known. I don't know whose shade it was; I called it Emilie. We are securely bound to one another, inseparably, though joined back to back.

This woman is my coffin. As she walks she conceals me within her guise. In cursing her I damn myself, and loving her, I fall asleep with a cast of her hand on my phallus.

On the first of May you'll go to the cemetery where in section ten you will find a woman sitting on a grave. She will be expecting you and will tell your future from the cards. You will leave to look for answers on the walls of boarding schools, but the heads of the young girls at the window will appear as buttock-buds and ass-tulips, quavering when a truck drives past. You will feel an intense fear lest they come crashing down onto the pavement, a fear similar to the pleasure you felt in childhood at your first convulsive erection and the terror you felt when your sister taught you to masturbate with her *tiny alabaster hand*.

From whom do you still expect solace? Emilie is in shreds, the fragments of her image have been dispersed by the wind to places unknown to you, and therefore you cannot now choose her as the instrument of your tranquility, not least because you have long time since stopped letting moments of parting distress you.

The heavens sleep, and somewhere behind the hedge a woman sculpted from raw meat awaits you. Will you feed her ice?

Klára always sat on the divan scantily clad, waiting to be undressed. One day she took the revolver from my nightstand, aimed it at the painting, and fired. The cardinal clutched his chest and tumbled to the ground. I felt sorry for him, and later when visiting the brothels on the city's outskirts and paying the whores for their prowess, I was always aware that I was buying a piece of eternity. Any man who has enjoyed the salty taste of Cecil's twat would sell his rings, friends, morals, everything to sate that monster hidden under the little pink skirt. O why can we never distinguish the first moments when women toy with us from those later moments when we cause them to despair?

One night I awoke just before daybreak, at the hour flower petals fall while birds are singing. Marta lay next to me, a repository of all the ways of love, a hyena of Corinth with her exposed vulva opening to greet the dawn. She caught my gaze, filled with revulsion, and I was sure that from the depths of her being she wished this horrid feeling of disgust on me. I saw her sex swell and spill out from her womb, increasing in size until it overflowed the bed and extended over the floor like lava filling up my room. I quickly got up and ran from the house like a madman. I stopped in the middle of a deserted town square. When I looked back, Marta's vulva, resembling a giant, monumental tear of unnatural color, was surging out my window. A bird flew up and pecked at my seed. I threw a rock at it to chase it off. "Be happy, you'll constantly replicate yourself," said someone walking past, then added, "your wife is now giving birth to your son."

Every day at noon two beetles would meet behind the pale blue corset of Our Lady of Lourdes. I came to the catacombs in complete innocence. A row of cubed chests naturally piqued my curiosity. Several boys, bound by their feet, were hanging head down in the crowns of olive trees, small fires roasting their curly little heads pink. In another room, I saw a cluster of comely naked girls knotted together into a single teeming mass, like a monster from the Apocalypse. Their vaginas opened mechanically, some vacant, others swallowing their own juices. I noticed one in particular whose labia moved like mute lips trying to speak, like someone's petrified tongue attempting to crow. Another smiled like a flower bud, and even today I would recognize it among a hundred preserved specimens. It was the sex of my dead Klára, who had been buried without being washed in the mint water she so loved. Despondent, I took out my cock and without a moment's hesitation impassively thrust it into that teeming mass at random, telling myself that vice and misfortune are always united by death.

Later I placed an aquarium in the window. In it I cultivated a golden-haired vulva and a magnificent penis specimen with a blue eye and delicate veins on its temples. Yet in time I threw in everything I had ever loved : shards of broken teacups, hairpins, Barbora's slipper, light bulbs, shadows, cigarette butts, sardine tins, my entire correspondence, and used condoms. Many strange creatures were born in this world. I considered myself a creator, and with justification. When I later had the box sealed shut, I gazed with pride at the putrefaction of my dreams, until the walls became so covered in mold it was no longer possible to see anything. Yet I was certain that everything I loved in the world existed therein.

Still my eyes needed something to feast on. They devoured nourishment voraciously, like a glutton, and digested it at night while I slept. Emilie spread scandal liberally, arousing lust in every being she met and conjuring up visions of her hairy orifice.

I remember another incident from my childhood. It happened around the time I was expelled from the gymnasium. I was scorned by everyone, only my sister would have anything to do with me. I would secretly go to her room at night. Lying in each other's arms, legs entwined, through long periods of absolute bodily quiescence we dreamed up that state of exhaustion that overtakes all who move along the razor's edge of *shame*. One night we heard quiet footsteps approaching. My sister motioned me to hide behind the sofa. Father entered the room, carefully closing the door behind him, and without saying a word lay down with my sister. I finally had a chance to witness how one makes love.

Emilie's beauty was not created to fade, but to decay.

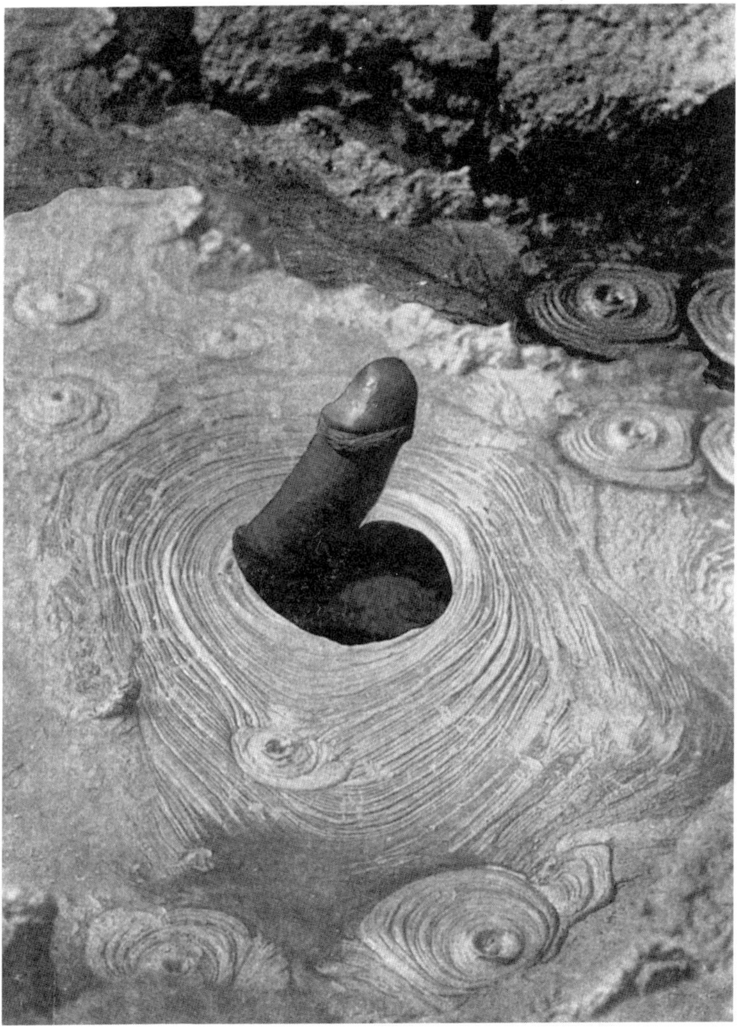

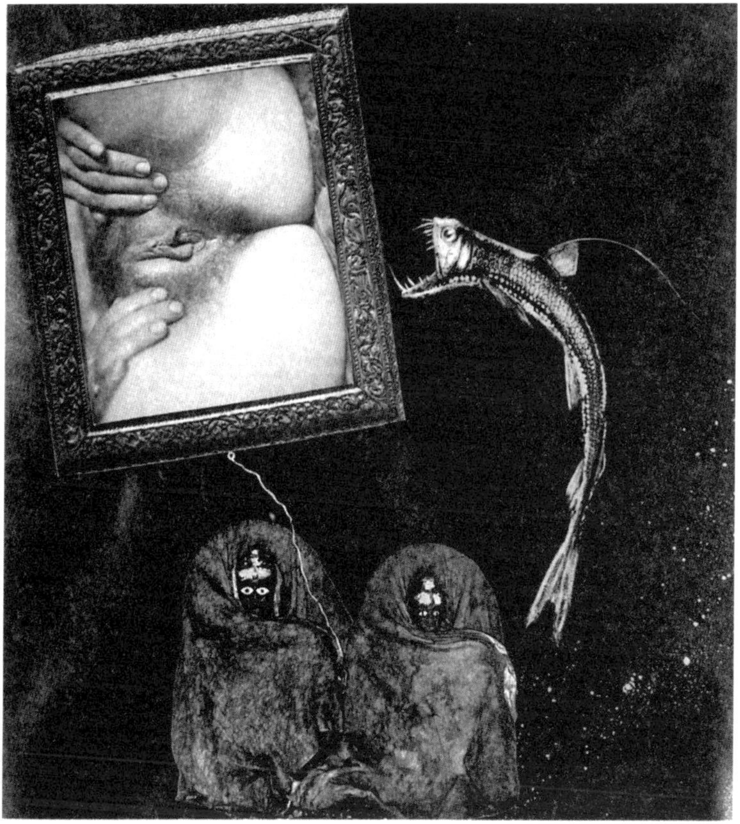

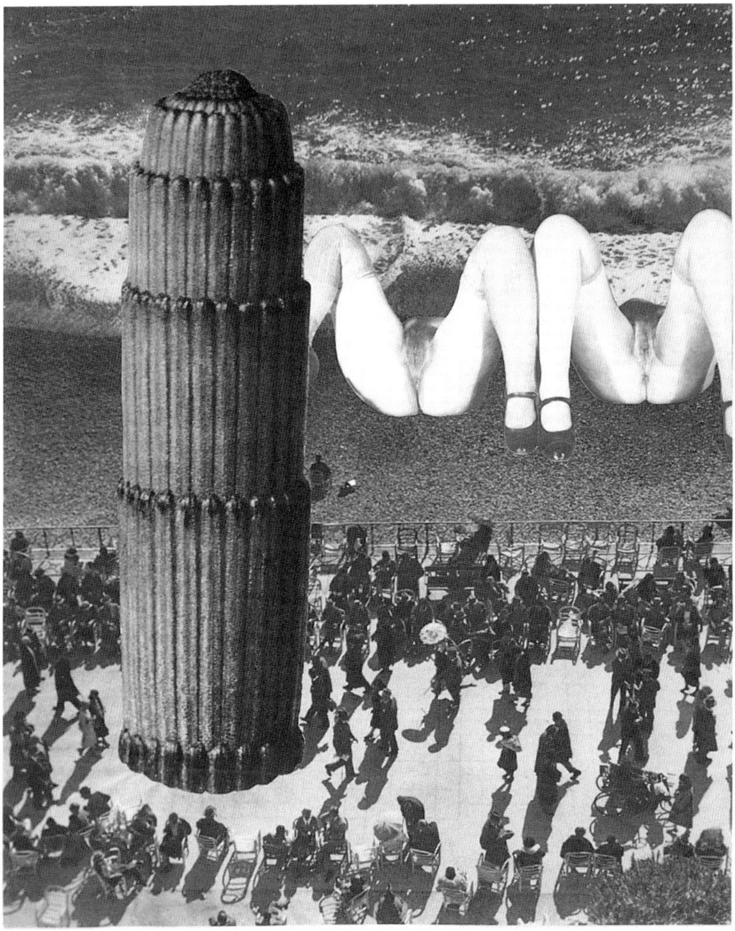

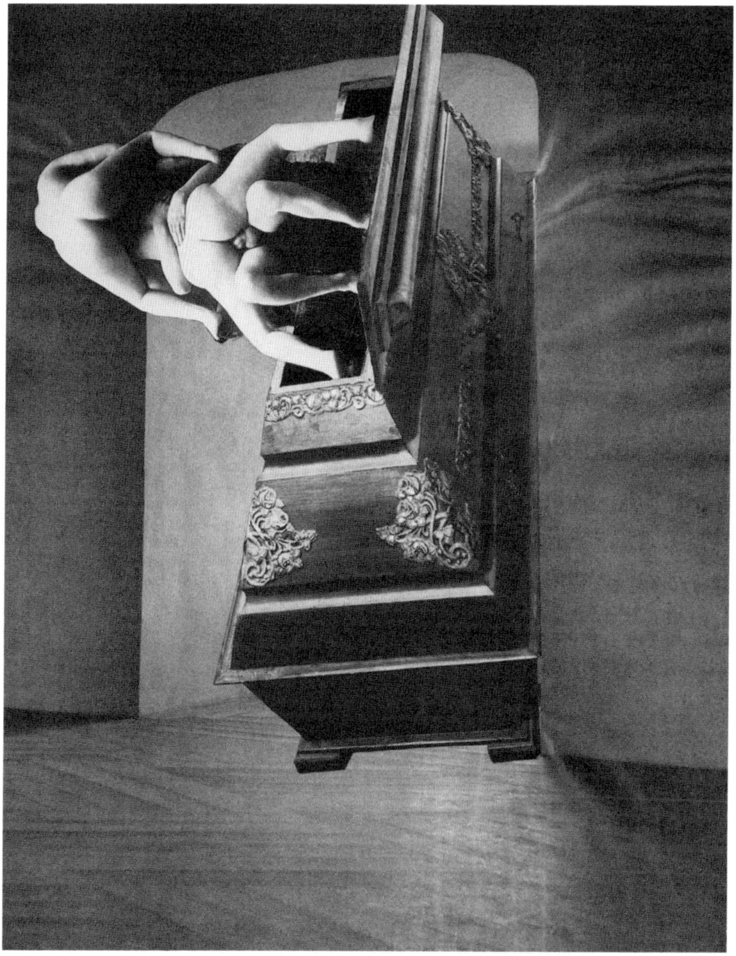

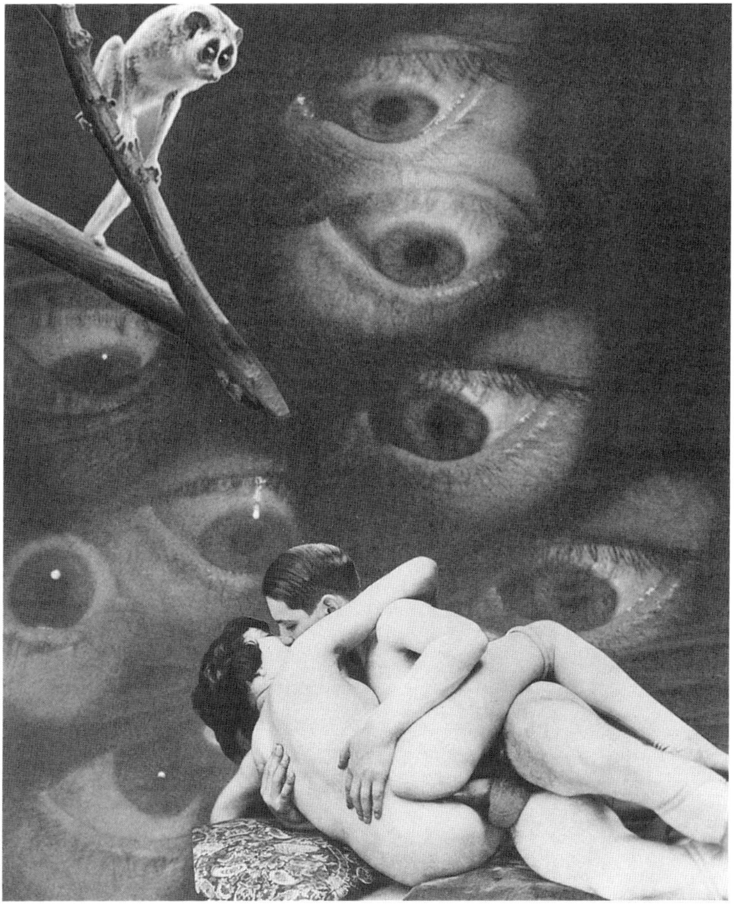

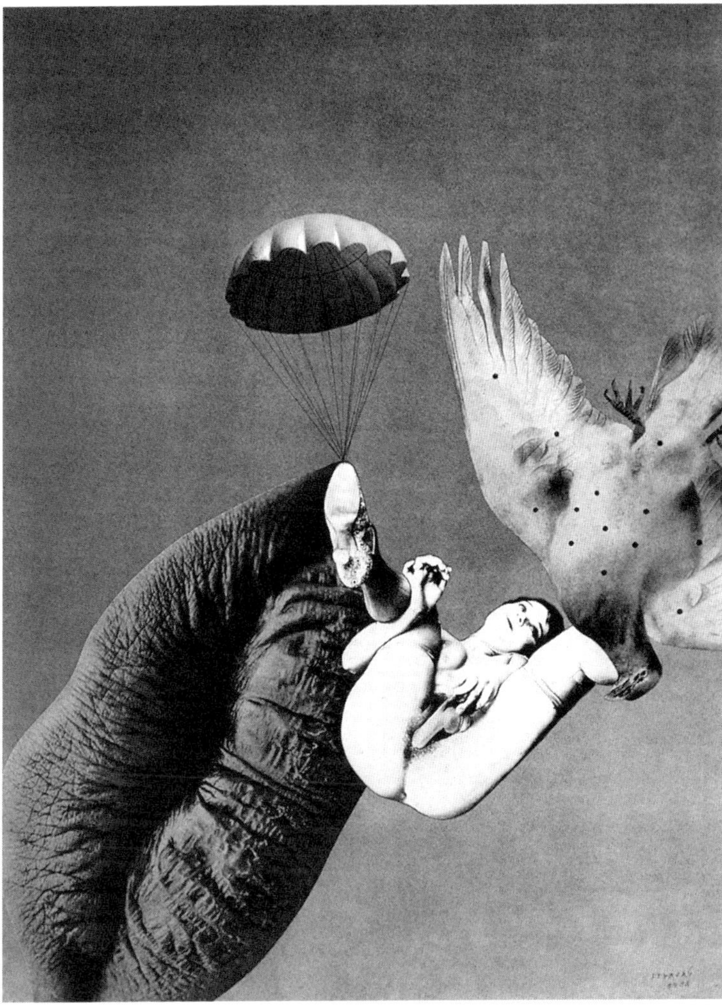

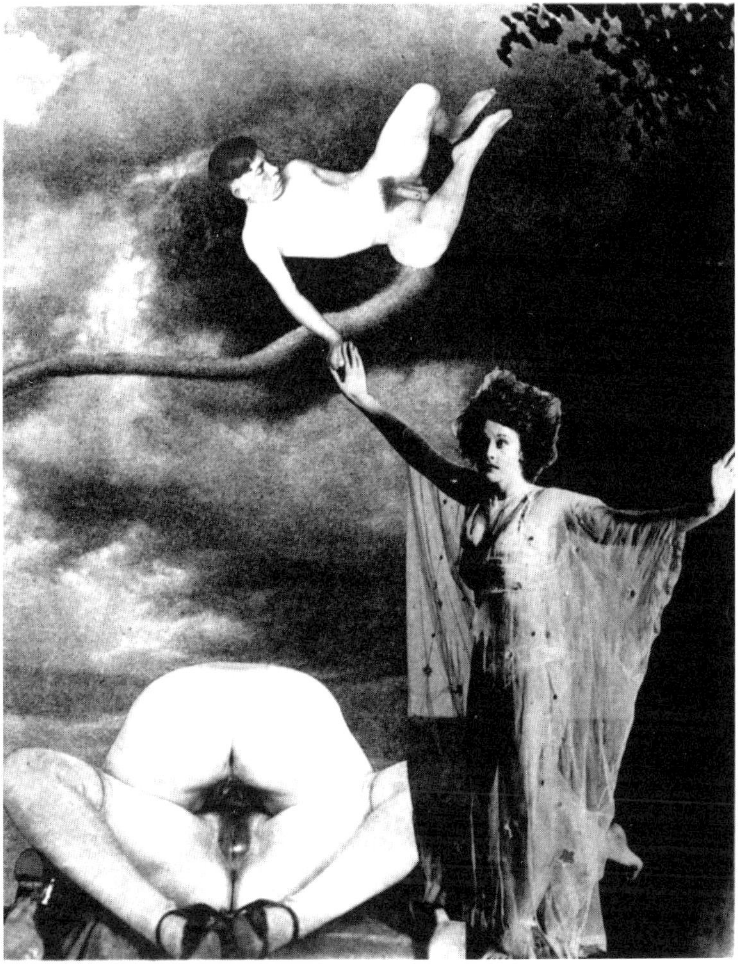

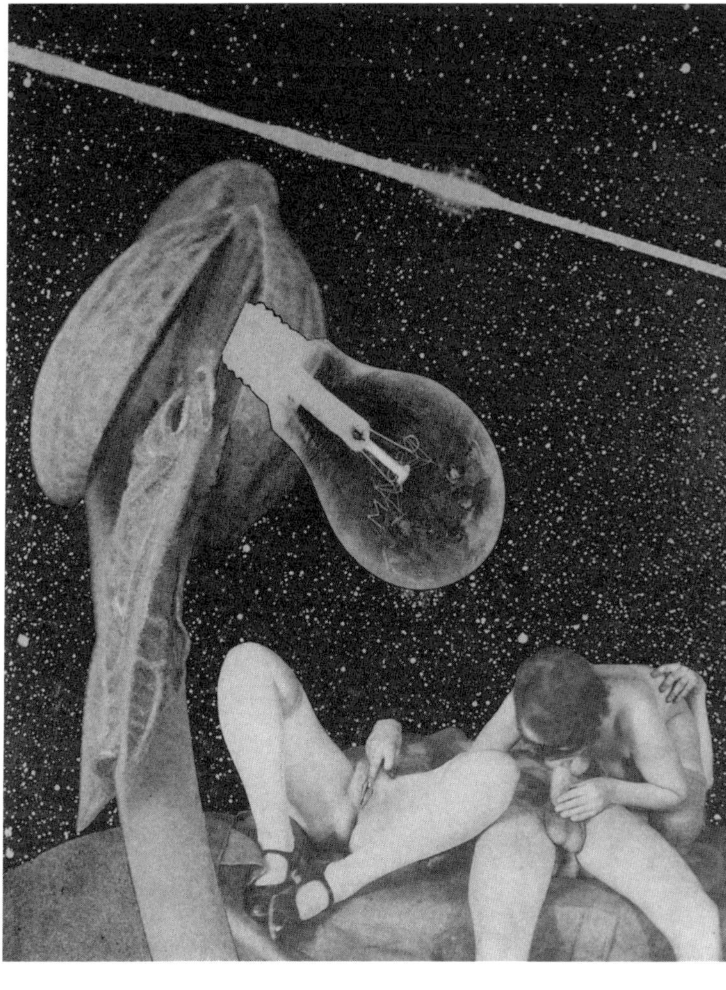

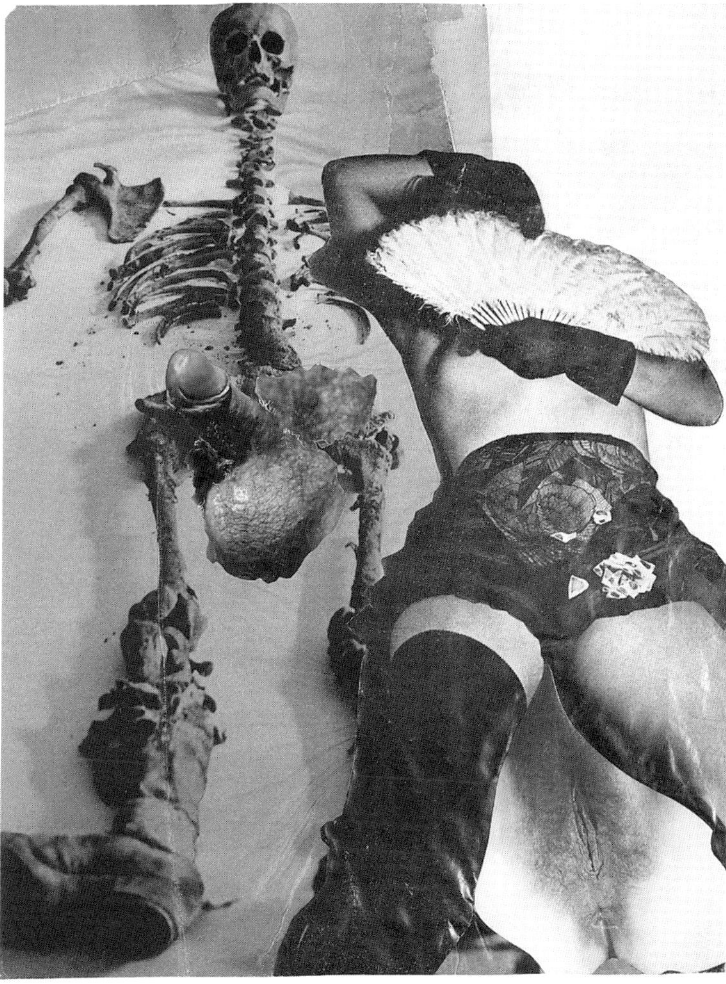

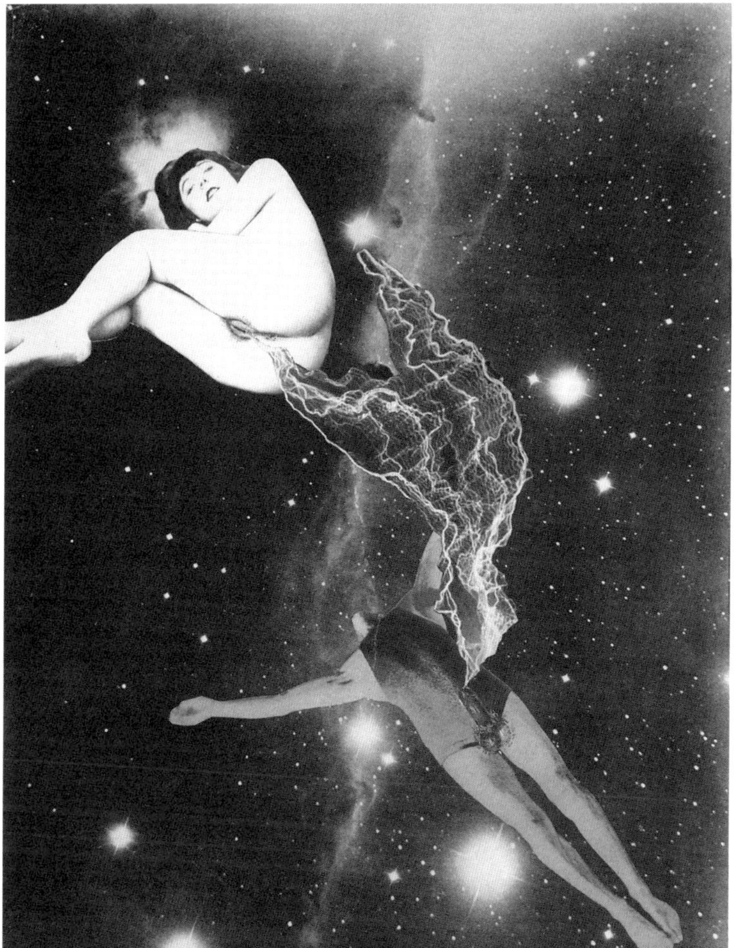

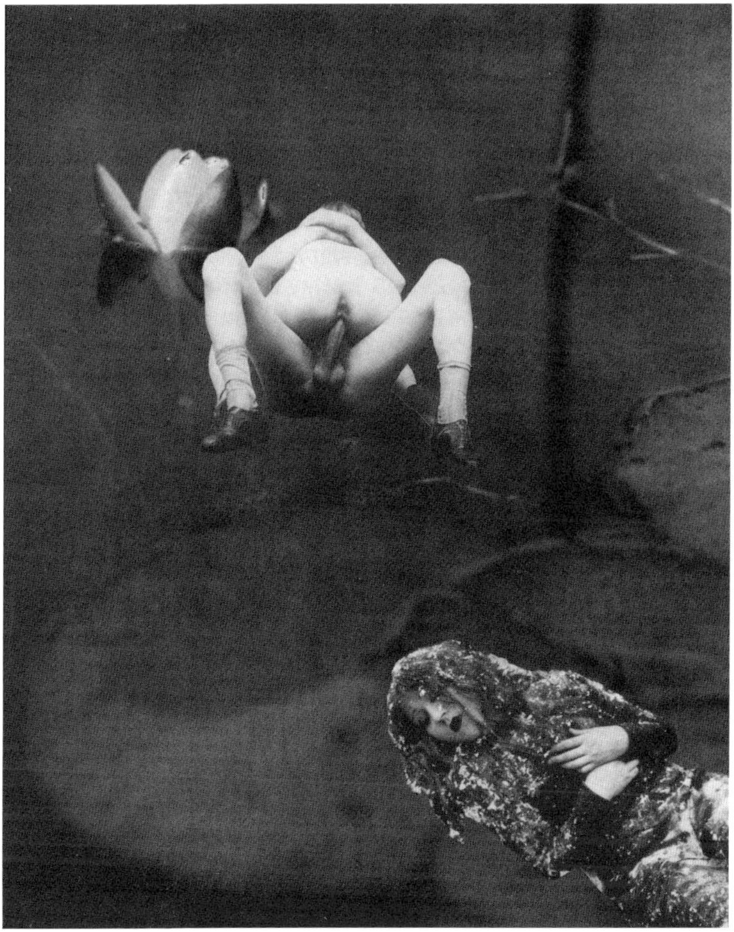

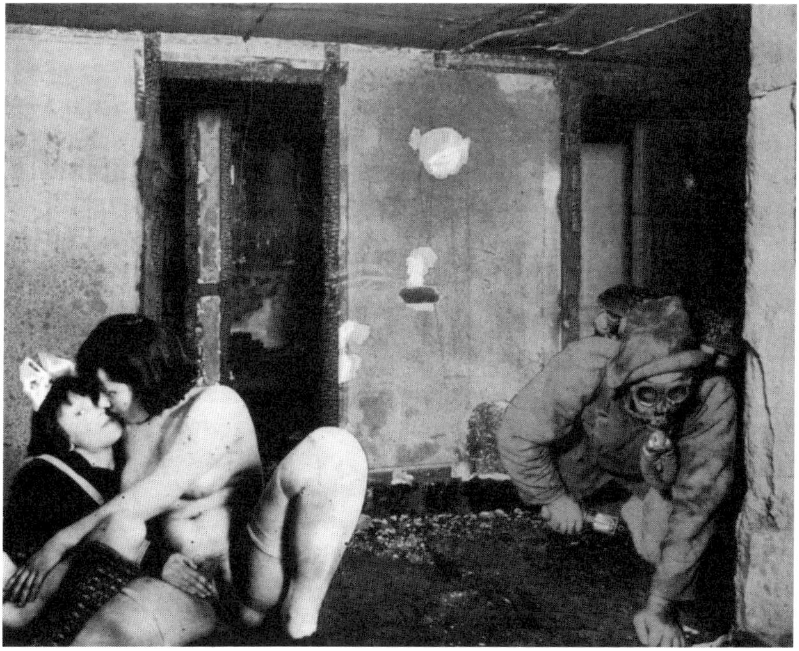

THOSE WHO CONCEAL THEIR SEXUALITY despise their innate abilities without ever having risen above them. Though they reject human mortality, they are incapable of liberating themselves from the lugubrious cycle of life — made possible and guaranteed by the genitals — to achieve the immortality of the mythical gods. And though they have created the illusion of their own immortality, thereby divesting their behavior and even their psyche of any sexual character, they will never eliminate the corporeal proof of their animality. The body will continue to demonstrate mortality as the fate of all humans, and for this reason any reference to human animality so gravely offends those who dream of its antithesis. They take umbrage not only at any mention of animality in life, but in science, literature, and the arts as well, as this would disturb their reveries by undermining their rationalist airs and social pretensions. Their superhuman fantasies are destroyed each and every time they are compelled to perceive acts both excremental and sexual, laying bare the vanity of their efforts to free themselves from the power of nature, which has, in assuming their mortality, equipped them with genitals and an irrepressible drive to satiate their hunger.

There is nothing as intensely dispiriting for those who have sublimated their corporeal substance than for their animality to spontaneously make its presence felt. Just consider how the signs of uncontrollable shits deject the hero during a triumphal campaign, or how painfully nabobs endure their sexual appetites toward despised subalterns. Nothing but the body pulls these haughty folk back to animality, disillusioning their superhuman self-confidence. The bodily processes they are unable to shake free of have become their Achilles heel, whose sensitivity has been superbly exposed by pornophiles.

The nature of pornophilia is at heart bellicose and

sadistic. Through their actions, pornophiles attack any mode of non-animality employed by others to elevate themselves over pornophiles. In pointing to human nature, they sweep away all pretensions of human inequality while at the same time proceeding from a new criterion : the creation of new castes distinguished not by social standing but by vital potency. Pornophilia thus collapses the illusions the high and mighty harbor of their divine nature while exposing their physical decrepitude, the inferiority that they have brought upon themselves through their contempt for the body. The body is the last argument of those who have been unjustly marginalized and ignored, because it demonstrates beyond question the groundlessness of all social distinctions in comparison to the might of nature. With the body, pornophiles not only abolish social barriers between people, through the vigor of the non-incapacitated body they also elevate themselves above those who in return scorn them from other angles. From this perspective, pornophilia could, above all, serve as a potent weapon for the socially powerless, the materially and culturally oppressed, who might, in this context at least, assert their strength and significance through the potency of their non-degenerate body. It is therefore understandable that those whom pornophilia attracts are of a more revolutionary bent than those mired in the prejudices of the moribund bourgeoisie.

Pornophiles use sadistic methods to attack the supercilious psyches of the ruling peacocks. Finding their dreams frustrated, those who are attacked counter in like manner with a sadistically motivated prudishness, a puritanical persecution of the "depraved." You can verify for yourself the reason for pornophilia's emergence : When in the company of these pompous snobs you will have the overwhelming urge to disrupt their prevailing idiotic idyll by roaring "shit, piss, fuck!" and so forth.

The primal reason for employing obscenity cannot be disguised even in the primitive expression of those barbarians who to this day draw the familiar diamond-shaped pattern and phallus on the walls of a metropolis. If the sadistic impulse of these displays is not directed at the socially smug, it is aimed at women, at their inferior, non-phallic sex organ, threatened with punishment by the penises represented in colossal drawings and sculptures. Present-day pornophilia — whose psychological value lies in the presentation of obscene works and expression, not in their neurotic concealment — has, however, become a weapon even against those of the same sex, unjustifiably puffed up though they may be. In other words, its features become more misanthropic than misogynistic.

Inasmuch as the biological consequences of one's sex ultimately has an adverse effect on pornophiles as well — since they, too, prefer to deny their mortality — the predilection for pornophilia assumes a particular trait that camouflages the general unpleasantness of being reminded of our animality. In this specific context, a work of obscenity may serve as a surrogate to sexual gratification, as a direct sexual charge. If inherently artistic, it will retain its militancy, albeit in a special sense. The sadistic character of pornophilic works, particularly those that are works of art, is of course usually latent, hidden in the artist's unconscious, without it ever reaching the level of consciousness proper, similar to what the vehement aversion puritans have for it implies. The true reasons for their behavior are as unknown to pornophiles as they are to puritans, and thus are erroneously interpreted. The sadistic import of pornophilic artworks naturally should not in any way impact their aesthetic evaluation, and it isn't any more perverse a motif than the reproduced motifs of customary genres.

In pornophilic works of art the sex is liberated from its actual biological function and envisaged purely in terms of pleasure devoid of its reproductive consequences, thus it does not attack the animality of the haughty per se but the relative inferiority of their animality. The artist does not provoke the puritan for their transience, their mortality, which the artist suffers as well, but for their impotence, their sexual inadequacy, which they have brought on themselves by leaving their *sexus* to degenerate through a foolish desire for superhumanness. By divorcing sex from its biological aspects and excreta from its content, pornophilic art does not conceal the sadistic nature of its stark obscenity, it merely curtails how its bellicosity is projected. Pornophilically motivated art, therefore, battles the haughty through sex's pleasure principle instead of through its biological purpose — in other words, what this art primarily attacks is imperfect humanity, not the imperfect divinity of the supercilious. The desire for immortality could be ridiculed for its baneful consequences alone, i.e., sexual degeneracy. Art, therefore, mitigates the sadism of pornophilia only in its exploitation of sex's biological function, which is as unpleasant to pornophiles as it is to pornophobes.

Yet pornophilic tendencies are found even in those who are actually maligned by pornophilia. They are especially fond of it as kitsch, whose purpose is sexual titillation. This mode of trash pornophilia completely attenuates the sadistic impulses of pornophilic art, which as a result renders it accessible precisely to that caste of people against whom it is essentially directed. Pornophilia has a corrupting influence solely on those puritans who persecute its bellicosity and sadism, having imputed to it the same meaning as their pornographic literature and pictures carefully hidden away in closed drawers until required for the occasional arousal, which as a rule their shabby wives can no longer produce. The only thing this sort of trash pornophilia does not need is a public, in fact, it resists one as any number of people, and not only puritans, find it difficult to reach orgasm in the presence of others.

We should, shorn of all prejudice, evaluate pornophilic works strictly on their artistic value. If anyone should think that obscene content in itself detracts from the value of a work of art, then we might just as well spurn the art of Strindberg or Tolstoy for its misogyny. Pornophilia cannot be reproached for being pathological as it is a disease of a similar order to any other manifestation of culture, no different even than the sadistic puritanism of its opponents. If pornophilia can be considered a work of art, it is as much a cultural phenomenon as "humanitarian" art, and if it limits itself purely to expressing the libido without any connection to other cultural or economic values, then it is no more neurotic than the trite expressions of compassion. Its pathological manifestations in erotomania and coprophilia are no different than the anthropophilia found in the masochism of martyrs. Our humanity, culture, and civilization are nothing more than an effective way to utilize neurotic conflicts. So until our pathologies give rise to works of value we simply cannot be taken to task for having this nature. The sublimation of the neurotic libido is creative, while the normal libido leads only to playfulness. Both libidos, therefore, participate in the creative process motivated by obscenity. The neurotic libido determines the work's content, while the form of its method is conditioned by the normal libido. If the normal libido looks to instant gratification for a surrogate, it will use obscenity to create kitsch, but if its needs are sublimated, then the result is a work of art.

The titillating, kitchified mode of pornophilic themes has no other value and function than that of an artificial doll designed for onanism (*ipsatio*). Such works are limited to the sexual act in and of itself and are incapable of disengaging from the atmosphere of the recess without ceasing to perform their function, which is founded on the illusion of coitus with a real partner. On the other hand, the artist whose work is not bound to reality sees no need to have naked girls urinate into a chamber pot when he could place them in an alpine valley instead. An ejaculation need not become a yellow stain on the bedding — it can be transformed into a bolt of lightning to cleave a Gothic cathedral. The bed of lovers can be replaced by the cosmos and the globe inserted under a woman's buttocks. And from her pudenda a sun then emerges, the most marvelous of miscarriages.

The artist not bound by the rational coordination of perceptions, real proportionality, and syntax exempts the sexual organ from its biological procreative function, which is perhaps too painfully evoked by pornographic kitsch when its titillating function ceases through the orgasm it has engendered. Artistic pornophilia can never be glossed by irony and cynicism as real or reproductive sexuality stuck to the bed sheets.

While a different world might have long ago achieved a transvaluation of art, the elaboration of sexuality has been impeded by the censorship of puritans who are incensed by obscene content insofar as it portrays healthy sex, whereas their sexuality is pitifully derelict under their flies. They are aware, even if unconsciously, of their sexual inferiority, and as their butts are deformed by hemorrhoids as well, they envy the formidable penises and unblemished rumps of others. What galls them to a far greater extent than pornophilic kitsch are works of art with obscene content, for here artists have extended the reign of their sex over the entire world. Kitsch pornophilia keeps to the realm of the recess. The artist, on the other hand, spans the entire world. They piss a sea, shit a Himalayas, give birth to cities, masturbate factory chimneys, etc. Nothing is sacred, everything linked via sexual association.

Their pansexuality carries a double meaning : the first attacks puritan impotence and the second frees sex from its procreative function. Here sex is comprehended in a purely aesthetic sense, voluptuously. The artist's pleasure, facilitated by the libido, is not dimmed by common veracity. The erotic scenes thus created do not stand or fall through an oppressive banality, although the banality and insipidness of sexual gratification cannot be eradicated by perverse appetites. These, too, are dull and banal. The libido needs a space to play in, a space that diverts the senses from the dismal post-coital condition and deters those rational speculations poisoning our pleasure. Our eroticism must be rid of its depressing connection to plump wives and conjugal beds under which a chamber pot lurks.

Nevertheless, as poetry is the art of finding the exotic in the mundane, there is no need to discard our inventory of the banal, only banal situations. This can be achieved only through a subjective evaluation of things and actions, liberating them from their customary hierarchy. Poetry negates reality's biological and economic meaning, annulling its rationalist context and creating a new syntax that gives old content new meaning, a new narrative. In this way the vapid, the graceless, becomes the exceptional, the emotive. Poetry is the art of discovering mundane life's emotive perspective. The art of living is the art of where and when to have a cup of black coffee, or in the sexual arts, where and when to orgasm. If puritans would like to call this a disease, then we shall help them. It is simply a matter of situational partiality.

From the world of dreams and hallucinations the modern artist enters the world of the most demented lunatics who are exhausted by the wayward adventure into which their reason has led them. Having renounced reason, the artist makes do with the adventure now presented by a libido liberated by liberated senses. The adventure of reason, of rationality, is pathologically sealed off by a psychosis that negates the intellect and by an autism that exempts us from rationally evaluating our observations and conduct. The liberated libido may autonomously reveal itself during this pathological state. Psychosis puts an end to the ravages of neurosis through negation, by gradually inhibiting mental and bodily functions. If psychosis is limited only to the negation of reason and does not inhibit perception, movement, and so on, then the natural channels for our emotional, aesthetic, and irrational actions and perceptions will eventually surface.

The world the demented arrive at through a numbness of mind the artist reaches through a soundness of mind, and thereby adopts a natural, purely hedonistic view of the real artistic possibilities that might be utilized. If ancient art is analogous to neurosis, then modern art is analogous to creative psychosis. The artist of today has emerged from the world of dreams, hallucinations, alcoholic deliriums, and violent, sweat-soaked, symbolic phantasms to an unaffected, purely emotive valuation and a perception of the real that spontaneously creates phantasms of the kind ancient art could scarcely imagine. Modern poetry has magically fanned out over all landscapes like the dream-like ambiance of an atelier. It has enabled the artist to disregard the socioeconomic values of life in favor of a thought and perception that are solely focused on pleasure. The liberated senses and psyche are thus able to see the entire world in its full emotive nature, albeit evanescent and momentary. Pornophilia as a work of art offers the pleasures of life far removed from pedestrian concerns. Having prudently rid our animality of its bleak vistas, the artist emancipates the acts of the body from their biological purpose, leaving us to revel in delight in a manner only granted by nature. Asceticism, any sort of renunciation of our sexuality, is unwarranted. As each person comes into the world at the end of an umbilical cord only inevitably to become dust, let us find pleasure in everything our abilities allow us.

BOHUSLAV BROUK

ORIGINAL COLOPHON

EDITION 69, VOL. VI, JINDŘICH ŠTYRSKÝ : EMILIE PŘICHÁZÍ KE MNĚ VE SNU

Postscript by B. Brouk. Privately printed exclusively for the publisher's friends, subscribers, and collectors in an edition of 69 copies. Nos. 1-10 (with 10 photomontages 13 x 18 cm) are printed on Pannekoek Holland and signed; nos. 11-69 (with 10 photomontages 9 x 12 cm) are printed on Simili Japan.

This book is not for public sale, nor available for loan, neither in public libraries nor disseminated in any other way. It should be kept in a secure location and out of the reach of minors.

TRANSLATOR'S NOTE

In 1931, Jindřich Štyrský introduced his new series of erotic literature and art in a promotional flier :

> Edition 69 will include works of outstanding literary merit and also be an album of graphic art that will have long-lasting value. Given the exclusively erotic nature of the work, the number of copies printed will have to be kept small, and it is my wish that these editions do not become the property of a wider readership, for whom they are not created nor intended. Quality was my sole guide when selecting from the work of contemporary and living authors. The very names of the poets, writers, artists, and translators should dispel any suspicion that I wish to disseminate illicit, pornographic trash anonymously and privately printed. Of the older literature, I have chosen works of unquestionable authenticity, even though they have continued to be ignored by official literary history on account of their ostensible immorality.

From 1931 to 1933, six volumes were published in the Edition 69 series, all illustrated : three from contemporary Czech authors and three translations from older works. The first, *Sexual Nocturne* (1931), the third, *Thyrsos* (1932), and the sixth, final volume, *Emilie Comes to Me in a Dream* (1933), were designed and illustrated by Štyrský himself. The other three volumes all appeared in 1932 : vol. 2, Marquis de Sade's *Justine*, illustrated by Toyen; vol. 4, a selection from Pietro Aretino's *Ragionamento*, illustrated by Toyen; vol. 5, a selection from Pierre-Jean-Baptiste Nougaret, illustrated by Rudolf Krajc. The series was conceived as a complement to the *Erotic Review* [*Erotická revue*], launched by Štyrský the previous year and also ceasing publication in 1933.

The influences that informed the conception for Edition 69 are varied. Nezval, Štyrský, Toyen, and Halas all were associated with the 1920s Czech avant-garde group Devětsil, which since 1923 had been operating under the twin rubric of Poetism and Constructivism. The former embraced literature, painting, and sculpture while the latter emphasized design (including book design) and architecture.

In his 1924 text "Poetism", Karel Teige, the group's leading theorist, outlined what Poetism is and isn't : "Poetism is the crown of life whose basis is Constructivism"; "Poetist art is casual, wanton, fantastic, playful, unheroic, and erotic"; "Poetism has no philosophical orientation"; "Poetism isn't literature"; "Poetism isn't painting"; "Poetism isn't an -ism"; "Poetism isn't art"; "Poetism is first and foremost a modus vivendi," and so on. What is important in this regard is that Poetism gave rise to the "picture poem" as its chief means of expression, a mode of collage that united literary association with Constructivist montage. Nearly everyone in Devětsil made them, and as Teige further noted : "The poetic image is the book illustration, the photograph, the photomontage." By the beginning of the 1930s, however, Poetism was beginning to wane and some of its members were already moving toward closer interaction with the French Surrealists, which culminated in March 1934 with Brouk, Nezval, Štyrský, Teige, Toyen, and others forming the Surrealist Group of Czechoslovakia, the first Surrealist group outside of France.

Other precursors of Edition 69 came from Paris. George Bataille's *Story of the Eye* and Louis Aragon's *Irene's Cunt* (an extract of which appeared in the *Erotic Review*), came out in 1928, both with illustrations from André Masson, followed by Max Ernst's first collage novels : *The Hundred Headless Woman* (1929) and *A Little Girl Dreams of Taking the Veil* (1930), which Nezval explicitly references in his text. Like Ernst, Štyrský used cut-ups of xylograph illustrations found in the pulp novels and periodicals of the day for his collages to "Sexual Nocturne."

The episodes in Nezval's contribution are more or less a true account from his time as a student in Třebíč, Moravia (the town of T.), where he was sent at the age of eleven. His experience with the prostitute is corroborated in subsequent autobiographical texts, where the brothel is conflated with other locations as in local idiom a brothel was ironically referred to as a "little café."

For Štyrský, the conflation of his dead half-sister, Marie, with Emilie, and in turn her merging with the other women mentioned in his text, mainly in the context of a sexual relationship, suggest a deeper stratum of the unconscious is at work. Similar to Ernst, Štyrský's sister died when he was six, and though the polarity of sexual pleasure and death was as central to his work as it was to Bataille's, according to art historian František Šmejkal, one of the first to give Štyrský's work critical attention, there was an even more direct connection to Ernst : "Štyrský created, even before he joined the Surrealists, his own myth of the phantom-woman, similar to that of Ernst, who transformed his dead sister into *The Hundred Headless Woman*." Štyrský explored this obsession in his dream journal (in the collection *Dreamverse*), notably in his Preface, "Dream of Emilie," and "Second Dream of Emilie."

Štyrský was one of the very first European artists to create illustrations to Lautréamont's *Les Chants de Maldoror*, preceding Salvador Dalí's more well-known work by five years. But interwar Czechoslovakia's censorship laws were rather severe, so when the Czech translation of *Maldoror* was published in spring 1929, with Štyrský's twelve colored lithographs, the censors immediately declared it "unsuitable for the public," and by summer much of the print run had been confiscated and other copies "sanitized" with whole sections blackened out. Not only did this cause an outcry in both Paris and Prague (Jaroslav Seifert, Philippe Soupault, Georges Ribemont-Dessaignes, and others wrote public protests), disgust at such prudishness also provided the motivation to launch both the *Erotic Review* and the Edition 69 series, though as the caveats on the colophons indicate, Štyrský was wary of overstepping the boundaries of the legally permissible.

While these texts are hardly shocking by today's standards, and even mild compared to the erotic prose of Bataille or Apollinaire, such themes were still taboo in Czechoslovakia's dominant middle-class culture. Symptomatic is Nezval's insistence on the words "fuck" and "bordello," which take on an incantatory magic,* as well as Bohuslav Brouk's tendentious assault on the bourgeois disdain for erotic art. Indeed, Brouk's work was often vociferously attacked by Czech critics, and it should be kept in mind that when he penned the Postscript

* The Czech word *mrdat* (which came to mean "fuck" in the 1890s), originally meant in Old Czech, much like the German *ficken*, "to move back and forth," "wag," or "wave." Mid-nineteenth century Czech-German dictionaries were favorites of Devětsil writers, and these are the "old dictionaries" to which Nezval is referring.

for "Emilie" he was still very young, though he had already published two books as well as numerous essays by then. Needless to say, his work was to have a lasting influence on Czech Surrealism.*

With respect to "Thyrsos," perhaps it's understandable that Halas considered this thin collection of poems juvenile and much inferior to his other work, which was indeed formidable (he won the State Prize for Literature in 1932, the same year *Thyrsos* was published). Yet it should not be dismissed out of hand. A few of the poems had already appeared in the first issue of the *Erotic Review* in 1930, and according to poet Ludvík Kundera, the collection could be viewed as an effort by Halas to overcome any self-censorship, and attacking censorship in all its forms was precisely Štyrský's raison d'être for these publications. So "quality," however defined, is not the issue here. As artists in far more repressive regimes than the democratic Czechoslovakia of the 1930s have always learned, the mere presence of zealous censors, or even social ostracization, usually results in the creation of works that accommodate automatically.

* One Czech critic disparagingly referred to Brouk's *Autosexuality and Psychoeroticism* (published by Surrealist Editions in 1935), as the "first Czech textbook on masturbation," while Jan Švankmajer cites it as the basis for his notorious masturbation machine.

In his essay "The Joys of a Book Illustrator," Štyrský notes : "An inferior illustrator approaches the work with the joint ambition to be a servant to the poet, the darling of readers, and a hit for the publisher. No illustration, save kitsch, is ever able to convey the idea of the work. Modern illustration accentuates the relationship between the *principle* of the work and its *formal expression* . . . [it] naturally adapts to the intention of the poetic work while retaining its own independent existence." The present volume was conceived as a way to display Štyrský's range as an illustrator by bringing together the three volumes of the Edition 69 series he designed with his own artwork. While his collages for "Sexual Nocturne" were in the spirit of Max Ernst, unlike Ernst he added elements of his own drawing to them. For "Thyrsos," he produced four simple line drawings as an elegant complement to Halas's ludic verse. And lastly, for "Emilie Comes to Me in a Dream" he created photomontages, the images sourced predominantly from French and German pornographic magazines. Ten were selected to accompany the text for the main print run of 69 copies, but a special printing included an additional two (reproduced here as the final two in the series).

JED SLAST
PRAGUE

FRANTIŠEK HALAS (1901 Brno – 1949 Prague) was one of the most important Czech poets of the 20th century as well as an essayist and translator. His major collections are from the interwar period. Active in the labor movement in his youth, he began publishing in the communist newspaper *Rovnost* [Equality] in the early 1920s and was editor of its youth pages. He co-founded the Brno section of Devětsil and published its magazine *Pásmo* [The Zone] from 1924–26, after which he became an editor at the Prague publishing house Orbis. Active in the resistance movement during World War II, he served in the Ministry of Information after the war ended.

VÍTĚZSLAV NEZVAL (1900 Biskoupky – 1958 Prague) was the leading Czech avant-garde poet of the interwar period. He was an early member of the pre-Surrealist group Devětsil as well as a founding figure of the Poetist movement. A prolific writer, his output comprises a number of poetry collections, experimental plays and novels, essays, and translations (most famously of Mallarmé and Poe). Having forged a friendship with André Breton and Paul Eluard, Nezval was instrumental in establishing the Surrealist Group of Czechoslovakia in 1934.

JINDŘICH ŠTYRSKÝ (1899 Čermná – 1942 Prague) was a painter, poet, photographer, collagist, and book designer, who also wrote essays and studies of both Rimbaud and Marquis de Sade. He became a member of Devětsil in 1923 and participated in their group exhibitions, serving as director of its drama wing, the Liberated Theater, in 1928–29. Štyrský was an active editor as well. In addition to the Edition 69 series, he edited the *Erotická revue*, which he launched in 1930, and *Odeon*, where many of his shorter texts appeared. He was a founding member of the Surrealist Group of Czechoslovakia.

BOHUSLAV BROUK (1912 Prague – 1978 London) was a founding member of the Surrealist Group of Czechoslovakia. Publishing his first study in 1930 at the age of seventeen in the avant-garde journal *ReD*, his work focused on interpreting the relationship between Freudian psychoanalysis and Marxism. Štyrský, Toyen, and Karel Teige designed the covers for the majority of his books, perhaps the most influential of which was *Autosexualismus a psychoerotismus*, published by Edice Surrealismus in 1935.

JED SLAST, a native of Richmond, Virginia, has lived in Prague for three decades. His translations include *Dreamverse* by Jindřich Štyrský, *The Tender Barbarian* by Bohumil Hrabal, and *A Prague Flâneur* by Vítězslav Nezval.

EDITION 69

František Halas
Vítězslav Nezval
Jindřich Štyrský

ARTIST

Jindřich Štyrský

TRANSLATION

Jed Slast

DESIGN

Silk Mountain

TYPOGRAPHY

Garamond Premier Pro

PUBLISHER

Twisted Spoon Press
P. O. Box 21 — Preslova 12
150 00 Prague 5, Czech Republic
twistedspoonpress@gmail.com
www.twistedspoon.com

EDITION

First softcover edition 2020, revised and expanded from the first hardcover edition published in 2004.

PRINTING & BINDING

Protisk, Czech Republic

TRADE DISTRIBUTION

Central Books
www.centralbooks. com

SCB Distributors
www.scbdistributors.com

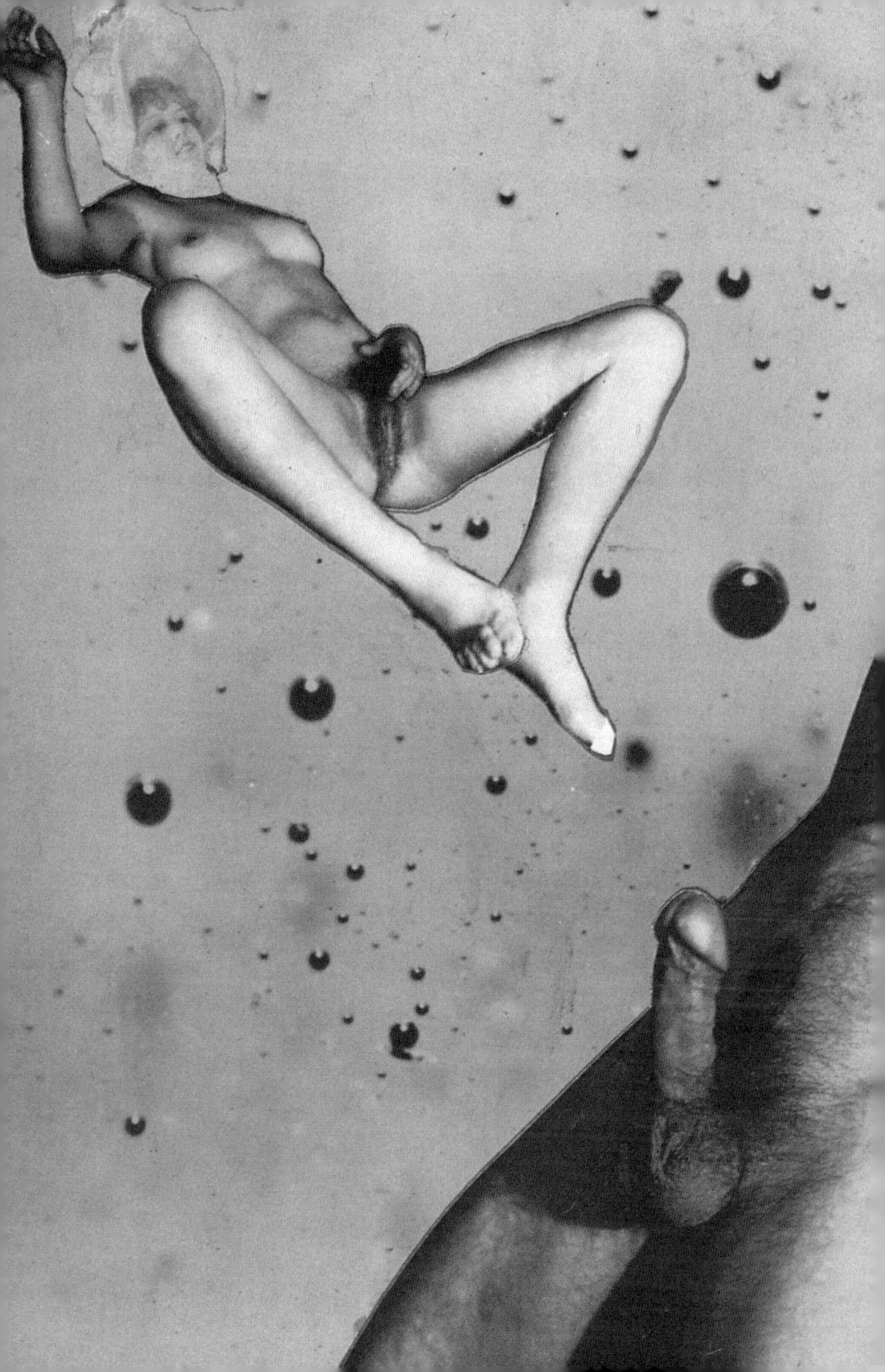